INTREPID ENCOUNTER

Rebecca Ashley

A CANDLELIGHT REGENCY SPECIAL

Published by
Dell Publishing Co., Inc.
1 Dag Hammarskjold Plaza
New York, New York 10017

Copyright © 1982 by Lois A. Walker

All rights reserved. No part of this book may be
reproduced or transmitted in any form or by any
means, electronic or mechanical, including photocopying,
recording or by any information storage
and retrieval system, without the written permission
of the Publisher, except where permitted by law.

Dell ® TM 681510, Dell Publishing Co., Inc.

ISBN: 0-440-14233-4

Printed in the United States of America
First printing—June 1982

**DEDICATED
TO**
*Angela Hovis,
and Vanessa,
Samantha, and
Becky Walker*

CHAPTER 1

"Couldn't we have just one more strawberry tart?" five-year-old Katie asked.

"Yes, please," her four-year-old sister, Julia, joined in.

The girls' pleading faces were upturned to their mother, but she turned an indecisive face toward the lady seated with them at the table.

"Mightn't they not, Caroline?" she asked, sounding like one of the children herself.

"Definitely not," Caroline said emphatically. "Katie has already had four and Julie has had three. I think that is quite enough for two young ladies who only pushed their capon about on their plates."

The disheartened children recognized defeat when they encountered it. But, not of a disposition to dwell on such minor setbacks, they turned their attention to slyly kicking at each other beneath the table. They were rather full, in truth, and Katie was not at all certain she could eat another bite, so a negative answer was not unwelcome.

"Why don't you girls run along back to the nurs-

7

ery and play?" Caroline suggested and their mother added her agreement.

As they stood and made pretty, if wobbly, curtsies, Trevina turned back to Caroline. "Perhaps I am too lenient with them," she suggested.

Caroline sighed. It was not a new topic. Trevina was definitely too indulgent with her children and the subject had already been discussed at some length. "Perhaps a little," Caroline agreed mildly.

"Charles was always so firm. There was not the least need for me to interfere with their discipline and I am loath to do so now," Trevina explained as if she were relating the facts for the first time, facts of which Caroline was well aware.

When Trevina's husband had died last year she had written a panic-stricken letter to Caroline demanding her help. She was, she wrote, totally incapable of managing *everything,* and her third nursery maid had just given notice. Why, even as she wrote, she informed Caroline in splotchy ink, she had now and again to take succor from the hartshorn that she kept ever handy. The children, she complained, were oversetting her something fierce and Caroline must come and take them in hand.

Not an ordinary letter, but Caroline, knowing the sender, had not been greatly perturbed. Her answer had been to direct Trevina to discard the hartshorn and instead keep a small switch ever handy—it was known to be much more effective in molding the behavior of children than hartshorn, whatever that particular product might promise against vapors.

Trevina had responded by writing that Caroline

was heartless and selfish and ended on a mournful note, declaring if Caroline could live with her guilty conscience after having rejected the plea of a poor widow, then Trevina wished her joy in her existence. She had closed with a melodramatic statement that she would not trouble Caroline further with her many heartrending concerns.

Caroline remembered her capitulation with a smile. She and Trevina had been friends since they had made their come-outs together seven years ago. Trevina might talk of severing ties but she would not. She would, rather, continue to inundate Caroline with letters reeking of violet and stained with little blotches that Caroline had often suspected were made by the writer flicking a wet hand over the finished letter, rather than being the tears they were obviously meant to represent.

But she had left her comfortable little house in Surrey and removed to Wiltshire to live with her friend, until, as Trevina solemnly promised, she was capable of handling her own affairs.

Trevina adjusted her lace around the neckline of her amber merino gown and steered the conversation into another direction. "I noted Mr. Wroxham paid particular attention to you at his mother's rout last night."

Her friend's sly, suggestive look was not lost on Caroline, who suppressed a gurgle of laughter. She had wondered what pretext Trevina would use to slip that gentleman's name into the conversation. Lowering her eyes demurely to hide her amusement Caroline replied, "Mr. Wroxham is always most kind and attentive to me as he is to all his guests. Did I not spy him talking to you on the balcony for a few moments?"

"We spoke for only a brief time." Trevina found her teacup a subject of interest as she spoke. She ran her finger around the edge of the dish before continuing: "He told me he would like to paint you sometime. He declares your large eyes are the perfect shade of hazel and your delicate features are very ethereal and would lend themselves well to canvas. Mr. Wroxham is a fine artist," she continued earnestly. "I am sure he would paint a very fine portrait of you, showing your curls as thick and copper-colored as they really are."

"Did he speak of painting you also?" Caroline asked with a look at her friend from beneath long lashes. Casually, she added, "He asked if your period of mourning was yet over and if it would be unseemly of him to call upon you."

Trevina looked at her with incredulous delight, an expression that was swiftly concealed and replaced by one of studied indifference. "I cannot think why he should ask such a thing."

"Give over, Trevina," Caroline cried, half in impatience and half in amusement. "It is *you* who holds his interest, as the most feebleminded person can see. You must not feel it is your duty to ignore all eligible gentlemen while applying yourself to seeing me married. There is not the least need for you to give him up for me; I find him a very amiable man, but I don't have an interest in him and you do."

"Oh dear, I must have been dreadfully obvious in

trying to attach you to him. And I so pride myself on being circumspect," Trevina lamented with a rueful smile.

"You *were* a bit obvious," Caroline agreed cheerfully, "but I know you mean well. I am simply not interested in marrying. After all, I had two Seasons in London and there were opportunities enough there to find a suitable mate had that been my intent. I did have a suitor or two," she reminded the other woman with a grin.

"Yes, of course you did," Trevina agreed stoutly. "The problem lies in the fact you did not choose to marry. Instead you returned to Surrey with nothing but that patch of garden in your tiny backyard to occupy yourself. It seemed terribly sad for you to live that way."

Caroline patted her friend's hand. "You are kind to worry for me but I assure you there is no reason to. I am perfectly happy being a decrepit spinster of four and twenty."

Trevina looked at her compassionately. "You cannot mean it. And you had not the least chance of meeting a suitable man in Surrey."

Caroline tried again with a smile. "I did not desire to meet such a gentleman. After all, I am not constrained to marry. The fortune I have may be small by your standards but it is ample for my simple life."

"That is not the point. Weren't you lonely?"

"I had my garden and books." Caroline skillfully avoided the question.

"I should have been dreadfully hungry for companionship and tediously bored," Trevina announced as she rose and walked from the room, the fabric of her amber gown making a gentle swishing as she moved.

Caroline smoothed the fabric of her own sky-blue cambric. She was only vaguely aware she did so; she was thinking back to her days in Surrey. She *had* been lonely a few times, she admitted to herself. It was, unfortunately, not a feeling that had been eased by coming to Wiltshire. Not that she did not thoroughly enjoy Trevina, she hastened to assure herself—it was just that every now and again it seemed as if there was something missing from her life. It was a silly feeling really, and one that always passed quickly. After all, she was surrounded by people who loved her and Trevina's family was very dear to her. What more could she want from life? Still . . .

Caroline reproached herself sternly as she caught the vision of the elfin figure of self-pity creeping into her thoughts. She was, she reminded herself, living in the lap of luxury and having to do very little or nothing if she chose to. It was ridiculous to complain about her lack of society. And that was silly in the extreme, for she knew several good women in the neighborhood and only yesterday she had enjoyed the nicest coze with Lady Bradley about that lady's recently married daughter.

A maid discreetly interrupted Caroline's thoughts, standing before her with a letter on a silver tray.

"What is it, Lilly?"

"Beggin' your pardon, ma'am, but you have a note."

"Thank you." Caroline picked up the letter opener and fingered the jeweled hilt as she slit the envelope. She extracted a letter and unfolded it.

> "Caro," it began, "I am so overset I can scarcely write but I shall force myself to since it is for the welfare of my darling daughter that I take pen in hand. Alas, all too soon her dear husband has died in the poor child's arms! It is imperative, I am certain you shall see, for you to journey to my dearest daughter with all due haste. I should, of course, go myself could I contrive to, but such is not the case. I shall not bore you with the reasons I am unable to remove to Dorset as I am certain you see it as your duty as an aunt to go to your dear niece and not question the grieving mother's inability to do so. Make haste, leave immediately! Fly!
>
> Georgiana"

Any other young lady, having received such an alarming missive, would have fainted upon the floor or indulged in a strong fit of the vapors. Such, however, was not the case with Caroline, who merely folded the letter neatly and drank the last of her tea. Standing with an air of resignation, she proceeded to the airy conservatory, where she found Trevina amidst a jungle of green potted plants. Her friend was carefully plucking some dainty ferns to add to a Wedgewood vase containing white roses.

"I shall have to go to Dorset for a short time," she said simply.

Trevina looked up in surprise. "Dorset, whatever for? I don't recollect your having any friends or relatives there."

"My niece, Melissa, lives in Dorset," Caroline explained and handed the letter to Trevina.

"Oh dear!" the other woman exclaimed after a quick reading. "This is by everything dreadful! The poor girl's husband dead! You must be prostrate with grief. And her dear mother unable to come!"

"I never met the man," she related logically. "I am sorry, of course, that he has died and that Melissa is left alone." Still, she could not truthfully say she was overwrought by the death of a stranger.

Trevina looked at her with glowing admiration. "You are always so strong. I can well imagine how it must strike at your heart to think of your poor niece consumed with anguish over the death of her beloved husband."

They had been married less than eight months and she did not think it had been a union made in heaven, but Caroline forbore to argue. Instead she said, "I cannot say how long I shall be gone but I shouldn't think it will be over a month."

"You must stay as long as you are needed," Trevina insisted. She patted her cheek. "And now I shall write dear Georgiana a letter expressing my sympathy." She set the vase on a table and swept out of the room.

Caroline followed more slowly, walking out into

the foyer and up the curving staircase to her large green and silver bedroom.

There she began to calmly lay clothes across the huge four-poster bed in preparation for her trip, not troubling to call her maid. As she packed, she thought about her forthcoming journey. It was not one she relished making, but there was nothing for it.

Melissa, her sixteen-year-old niece, had married the earl of Devlon, a rich man in his late forties, only recently. The earl's death, while something of a surprise, was by no means a source of grief. Caroline had never met the earl but she had strongly disapproved of the marriage of two people of such differing ages—to say nothing of their differences in background.

Melissa had traveled around Europe almost like a gypsy with her mother, who had lived with a fair number of noblemen on the continent at one time or another. Now Georgiana was residing in Ireland with a baron. One of her few letters to Caroline had expressed the hope he might marry her. After all, Georgiana had pointed out, hadn't Hamilton made Emma his lady after years of living together? Caroline had suspected from the moment she read her sister's missive that Georgiana's inability to travel to Dorset must mean the baron was close to coming up to scratch. If that were so, then Georgiana wouldn't want anything to interfere with her marriage prospects.

As Caroline carefully folded a gray poplin dress and stacked it neatly on the brocade coverlet of the bed, she thought of Melissa. She had not seen her niece since she had endeavored to have Melissa reinstated in Miss Pinkerton's Academy for Young Ladies. That had been immediately after Melissa had been caught climbing out a window to have an assignation with a street lighter in Chiswick Mall. The project had met with no success—neither the reinstatement nor the assignation—so Caroline had sent the thirteen-year-old girl back to her mother, who was in Naples at the time.

Melissa, surprisingly, was a biddable child. Her personality was pleasant and she was a sweet if dull girl. Her only lamentable habit seemed to be the one she had inherited from her mother—the penchant for dallying with gentlemen. Where and when Melissa had met the earl, Caroline had no idea, but after a very brief acquaintance they had been married.

Well, Caroline thought, she owed it to Melissa to go to Dorset and take matters in hand. Unless she sorely missed her guess, her niece was unable to manage a large house and estate and would welcome the assistance.

Trevina entered as Caroline searched through her japanned desk for books to pack. "I realized it was thoughtless to abandon you in your hour of grief," she said.

Caroline looked up with a quick smile, then bent back to a study of the titles. "I am taking some improving books with me. Do you want me to leave any for you?"

"No, I'm waiting for Harriette's memoirs to come out before I read an improving book," she giggled.

"The *on-dit* is that she is going to tell all about her affairs with Wellington and Lorne and every *ton* gentleman who had her in keeping and is too clutch-fisted to buy himself out of her book. It should be delicious!" She smiled in anticipation of the indiscretions the book would reveal.

"I don't think *that* is an improving book," Caroline said with a laugh. "Nor do I blame the duke for refusing to be blackmailed. Although, I daresay, it may contain some improving passages for married couples looking for ways to enliven their marriage."

"Shocking," Trevina said in accents she tried to make severe, but her smile belied the fact she certainly hoped the book contained *all* there was to be said of life between the sheets of London's leading demi-rep of five years ago.

"Apropos to marriage," Caroline's hazel eyes danced mischievously, "I wonder if Georgiana's inability to go to Dorset means she has finally trapped that baron into making the trip down the aisle?"

"Georgiana would never seek to entrap anyone," Trevina denied.

"She would the baron," Caroline replied candidly. "She's been angling for him for over two years. That's the longest she has ever lived with any man."

"My dear," Trevina objected, "it's terribly indiscreet to say that your sister is living with a man. People will form altogether the wrong opinion of your family."

"Well, they will have the right idea about her," Caroline noted as she laid out a neat row of kid gloves on the bed beside the books. "And if my saying she lives with men is indiscreet, then it can only be more so of her to do such a thing."

"Does the fact overset you?" Trevina asked kindly.

"Oh no, I find it a source of some amusement," Caroline confided, her hazel eyes lighting with another quick laugh.

"You are incorrigible," the other woman said firmly. "I don't doubt any number of gentlemen would be shocked to hear you speak of such indelicate matters."

"No, any number of men would *pretend* to be shocked. When I find one who wouldn't, I shall marry him," she offered largely.

"Careful, Caroline," Trevina warned laughingly. "You have no idea whom you might meet in Dorset."

CHAPTER 2

"I have always been partial to plum pudding," Annie said, crossing her small hands placidly in the carriage seat beside Caroline. "That's not to say I don't like chocolate puddings, for I'm ever so fond of them, as I am equally favorably disposed toward strawberry syllabubs. Although, I have, on occasion," she admitted, "found them to be a bit on the tart side—just a wee bit, you understand."

Caroline's eyes skimmed the tiny woman beside her with a sideways glance. Her companion was dressed, meek and mouselike, in a slate-gray dress with a fitted bodice and bell-shaped skirt. On her lap she held a dove-gray cloak that was of the same unremarkable style as her pearl-gray bonnet. That particular article tied severely beneath her chin to give her small, wrinkled face the appearance of a child muffled for winter.

With her dove-gray cloak included, Caroline suspected Annie could not have weighed over seven stone. She was a thin, almost wizened specimen of aging spinsterhood. But could one have been listening to Annie's conversation without benefit of seeing her, they would most certainly have guessed her to push the scales to the same weight as a Hereford cow, and a good-sized one at that.

When Caroline's own maid had fallen ill at the last minute, Trevina had insisted Caroline take her maid, Annie. Caroline had accepted out of necessity. Now, she was discovering, Annie had two ruling passions, food and superstition. And she talked of both of them incessantly.

"I don't doubt that we shall be treated to any number of delightful desserts at Hollowsby," Annie anticipated gleefully.

"I'm certain we shall," Caroline agreed mildly and then turned to look out the window, a subtle hint that she wished to be left in silence with her thoughts.

Outside, the countryside was sliding past with the crisp clarity of scenes in a Donowell painting. The landscape of lonely villages set against the vast Salisbury Plain had gradually given way to the pleasing diversity of Dorset. The road threaded along beside a quiet stream, leaving behind the somber heaths of heather and bracken as firmly as it had earlier deserted barley and wheat farmlands populated with giant oaks.

Dorset was vastly different from Wiltshire, Caroline noted. It was a study in contrasts, ranging from lush vales of pastureland to the richly wooded lands that stretched onward toward empty moors dotted with scrub oak and silver birches. Caroline was quite enjoying the variety.

She had been to Dorset only once, and that was

when she was seven, but she was well acquainted with it. She had read a good deal about it in the few months she had spent with Trevina. It was not that Caroline had been possessed of any burning desire to learn about Dorset; it was simply that there had been very few books in the library and a travel book to that particular shire had happened to number among them. At Trevina's there had been time enough to read in the quiet evenings after the children were abed. She suspected she would not have that luxury at Melissa's, as there would be too many matters to attend to.

At least, she considered, as she let her eyes drift closed and felt the steady hum of the carriage wheels lulling her to sleep, she would have a day or so to rest after she reached her niece's house. A competent staff of servants would have everything in firm control, leaving her and Melissa time to make the important decision of whether the young girl should continue to reside in Dorset or sell the estate and go somewhere else to live. In either event, it would be imperative to find a suitable companion. Or Melissa could remove to Ireland to be with her mother.

Caroline smiled wickedly at the thought of Georgiana's reaction should Melissa arrive in Ireland to live with her and the baron. Knowing Georgiana, and Caroline fancied she knew her older sister quite well, it was possible she had even neglected to mention to her baron that she had a daughter at all. And if Georgiana had spoken of a child in passing, she had doubtless implied Melissa was still in leading strings—certainly not old enough to be married.

Snuggling back against the squabs, she put all thoughts from her mind and gave herself over to the lulling music of the wheels. Gradually she drifted off to sleep to savor dreams of being merrily chased by large sweetmeats, treats that matched the thorough descriptions Annie had given. It was an altogether pleasant dream except that Caroline awoke feeling quite ravenously hungry. Her auburn curls, which had been confined within a white poke bonnet, had escaped their prison when the bonnet slipped off while she slept. She picked up the hat from the seat beside her and tucked the silken strands firmly inside, brushing back a few errant wisps before tying the ribbons.

Annie, perceiving her mistress was awake, began again where she had lost her attention. "I'm very grateful to have the opportunity to come to Dorset with you, ma'am." As she spoke she searched in her reticule for a receipt of a dessert she had written out and particularly wished to show Caroline. "It's a pity your own maid was unable to come, but I don't mind leaving Mrs. Austin and the dear little girls for just a short space of time. I did, after all, plant a marshmallow by the house for good luck so they will be quite safe."

She triumphantly pulled a wrinkled scrap of paper from her battered reticule and held it up. "Ah, here it is. You see, you begin with one pound of loaf sugar. That's very important because if it is added later I think the flavor is impaired somewhat."

Caroline took the receipt presented to her and pretended an interest in the contents of a compote of apple. Why was she so ferociously hungry when she had eaten not two hours past? Glancing out the window, she thought she could just spy the top of a house showing over the crest of a hill. Surely they would be at Hollowsby shortly where they would be greeted warmly and offered tea complete with scones, cakes, and sweet bread. Her mouth watered at the thought.

A moment later the carriage rounded a bend in the road and Caroline saw the handsome facade of a Greek revival house in red brick. A hip roof capped the large three-story structure and was pierced by twin chimneys, one on either side of the long house. A pediment and portico of winter white added a finishing touch to the stateliness of the house.

In the distance behind the house, Caroline could see Golden Cap. It was one of the highest peaks in the shire—or so her guide book had claimed—and the most majestic. Caroline was inclined to agree with that description now as she gazed in awe at the varied colors of the cliff. A gray-white rock formed the base and edged upward into a dramatic blue-black layer and finally the yellow top. With the sun catching the peak, it glowed as golden as a guinea coin.

The carriage halted with a gentle sway and Caroline focused her eyes back on the house. It was a graceful-looking edifice, she acknowledged grudgingly. At least taste must have run in the family somewhere, even if the last earl had been a reckless man with the bad judgment to wed a child young enough to be his daughter. Caroline was just as glad that she had never met the man, for she didn't think she could have kept a civil tongue in her head to him. Admonishing herself that she should not think ill of the dead, she put all unkind thoughts of the late earl from her mind.

After the postilion opened the carriage door and the steps were let down, Caroline alighted to a pebbled driveway and walked up the wide set of steps to the front door. She knocked and waited for it to open. When it did not, she pushed it ajar, exchanging a look of surprise with Annie as the hinges groaned in protest.

"I don't think we should go in," Annie said, eyeing the house with an uncertain look. "The door is trying to tell us to stay out."

"The door is trying to tell us it wants greasing," Caroline said dryly as she stepped inside.

She looked around curiously at the rotunda-shaped room she found herself in. The marble floor had carefully cut blocks radiating out, sunlike, from a round center. Overhead, beams in Tudor arches accentuated a high ceiling. Across the wide expanse of the room, stairs of eggshell travertine marble made a grand ascent to the second floor. To the left and right, wide hallways departed to the two wings of the house. Furniture of some antiquity was lined about the walls of the round entryway. A carved table in heavy dark wood flanked a recessed window. On the other side of the window was a massive Plantagenet bureau and a Spanish clock with silver pendulum that swung ponderously back and forth. Completing the furnishings were heavy green brocade drapes that hung in looping swags over the windows.

The overall effect was that of elegance preserved just a bit too long. The faintest scent of musk hinted of carpets long unturned and badly in want of airing. The green curtains were on the point of fading, chameleonlike, to a yellow green.

"Whatever do you make of it?" Annie whispered beside her, her voice echoing in the vast hall. "It looks as if it ain't been inhabited these last score of years."

"I quite agree," Caroline said, startling herself as the sound of her voice reverberated in the massive chamber of the room.

"Shh," Annie cautioned. "You'll raise the house."

"And so I expect to," Caroline retorted, recovering herself enough to feel a creeping sense of irritation, augmented by an uneasy sensation of having ventured into someone's private cemetery. Why was no one here to greet her? Where were the servants?

For answer she heard the faraway sound of voices arguing in loud tones.

"I shan't answer the door and there's an end to it," a woman's voice proclaimed. "It's not my affair that the butler and the footman both gave notice and shabbed off within a day's space of each other. I'm the housekeeper and not the doorman. I'll thank you to remember that."

For reply a man's phlegmy voice responded with a rasp. "Demme, I'll not be the one to be forever hyin' up and down them steps. I'm that tired from doin' all the gardenin' and bein' the butler all in one.

25

And I ain't the one to be assumin' the job of openin' doors. You're the one seen the coach pull up so you be the one to answer the door."

Annie exchanged a glance with Caroline and moved back a step toward the door. "Perhaps," she said in hushed tones, "we should just be going along. We could stay at an inn tonight while you send a note to let your niece know where you are," she added hopefully.

"Nonsense. I had informed Melissa I would be arriving today. It is just now three o'clock, the exact time I told her I intended to be here. We are expected," she finished firmly.

Annie appeared skeptical at this knowledge. Her look quickly changed to one of fear as the first groundshaping peals of the clock began to sound, verifying Caroline's claim of the time as it shook the house to its very foundations.

"Merciful heavens!" Annie whimpered. "Let's be gone from this unholy place. I feel certain it's bewitched."

"Don't be a goose, Annie. We just heard voices."

At that reminder Annie's eyes widened further. "Yes, but were they the voices of living people?"

"Annie," Caroline replied briskly, "that's quite enough. Since I don't see a bell rope we shall simply have to go in search of someone if we do not wish to spend the remainder of our visit standing in this drafty hall."

Caroline marched up the stairs, her kid shoes making slapping noises on the marble steps. Annie followed behind her, taking exaggerated care to make no noise and quietly beseeching Caroline to do likewise.

"I am persuaded it is a haunted house. The ghosts will be angry with you for disturbing them with such loud noises," Annie warned as they reached the top step.

"Fustian!" Caroline retorted with spirit as she stopped and peered down the length of the two long wings that led off in either direction. She was on the point of starting down the west wing when the front door opened again. Both women turned and watched in surprise as a man entered.

He did not see them but Caroline had a clear view of him as he stalked into the round room below. He was a tall man wearing a dark, many-caped great coat that billowed behind him as he walked. His shiny black boots thudded with heavy intensity, breaking into the silence of the house with a deafening noise. But it was his face that immediately attracted Caroline's attention. It was set in hard lines with black slashes of eyebrows and a firm, taut mouth. And the windblown ebony hair that capped his head gave the man an almost fearsome appearance.

Behind her, Caroline heard Annie gasp. "He looks like the devil himself," Annie whispered.

At that instant, the man stopped in the center of the room and looked up the staircase. His black frown deepened as he saw the two women.

"Is this the usual way you greet visitors?" he demanded. "Well, don't just skulk at the top of the stairs, come down here."

As they hesitated, he continued, "Ah." His voice changed to a sardonic contempt. "Don't be alarmed. I shan't eat you, you know. Do come down."

"Don't do it," Annie advised.

Caroline gave her a damping look and began a slow descent down the stairs, regarding the stranger with haughty dignity. She reached the bottom step and stopped. It was a move calculated to leave her at the stranger's level. Unfortunately, he was even taller than she had thought and she was obliged to look up to him, even from her vantage point of one step.

He crossed the remaining distance to her and bowed formally. When he rose, a mocking expression lightened eyes that were a surprisingly deep shade of blue—like the ocean under a cloudless sky.

"So you are the young lady that Chester married? I must confess you are a trifle older than I expected. No offense, of course," he added in a tone that Caroline suspected was very much meant to give umbrage. "I had been given to understand you were a girl still in your teens," he continued calmly, regarding her as if she were a prize specimen at a country fair. "Still, Chester's taste was never at fault and I see he maintained his high standards to the end."

His leisurely appraisal of her body, lingering at various points along the way, caused Caroline's bosom to heave with indignation, a fact that did not appear to go unnoticed by the stranger.

"I thank you for your compliment," she said acidly, "but I was not Ches— the earl's wife."

"No?" he asked with one dark eyebrow raised in

interest. "Really. Then I am surprised he would have brought you to his house. And with his wife in residence."

The color flamed in Caroline's face. "I was not his lightskirt either, sir!"

His eyebrow quirked again and Caroline gave him a darkly suspicious glance at the trace of amusement she detected in his eyes.

"Indeed. Then, whom do I have the pleasure of addressing?"

"I am Miss Caroline Norton, Melissa Courtney's aunt. *She* was the late earl's wife."

He perused her face with interest. Then he straightened and adopted a formidably aloof position, the last vestiges of humor gone from his face. Caroline was tempted to back up a step to put her farther away from the odious man, as well as to raise herself to his height.

"Ah, a redoubtable aunt. How very convenient."

"And this," Caroline continued grandly, wishing to put the man out of countenance altogether by proving that everything about her was entirely correct, "is my maid, Annie Darby."

Annie, lingering halfway up the steps, clung ferociously to the marble balustrade when the man turned his gaze on her. She attempted a curtsy but managed only to sway back and forth. Her eyes remained fastened on him with a fearful look.

"Annie," Caroline motioned peremptorily, "do come down here. There is not the least need for you to wait on the steps."

While Annie began a reluctant descent Caroline

turned back to the stranger and gave him an arch look, shot through with a liberal dose of condescending hauteur. "And whom, might I ask, are you?" She lifted her delicately arched brows in question.

"I am the earl of Devlon."

"Merciful heavens!" Annie squealed. "The earl himself has come back! I knew the house was haunted!" She promptly fainted dead away.

CHAPTER 3

Lord Devlon caught the older woman in one swift movement. His boxing agility came in handy in the most unexpected places, he considered wryly, as he swept her off her feet before she hit the hard marble of the floor. Carrying her weight easily, he started from the round entryway bound for the west wing parlor.

He strode toward it while the other woman scrambled after him. As he entered the room, he noted with a grimace of distaste that the heavy furniture he had always disliked still embellished it. Cumbersome pieces upholstered in midnight blue and the lighter blue damask of once-lavish draperies still bespoke the grandeur of bygone days. Here, too, he smelled the musk and rotting cloth odor that had assailed his nostrils the moment he had entered the front door. The whole damned house was decaying before his very eyes.

"Where are you taking her?" Caroline demanded.

He ignored her question as he placed his light bundle on a couch by the window. "Give me your hartshorn," he barked.

"I haven't any."

He looked up at her impatiently. All the women he had known, and there had been a great many of them, had carried hartshorn in their reticules. This woman seemed intent on being perverse.

"I haven't the least need of it," she added, seeing his look of exasperation.

"Then find some," he commanded.

She gave him a sour look but moved to obey. Crossing to a tasseled bell rope that hung in the corner, she pulled it. As she tugged upon the ancient fabric it gave a weak resistance and then collapsed in her hand. Caroline stood holding the bell rope and looking at it in some bemusement.

"Never mind the restorative," he called. "She's coming around."

Caroline gave one final look at the bell rope, tossed it onto a carved Stuart table and hurried back to Annie. Her maid blinked owlishly, focused on the stranger, and blinked again.

"It's all right, Annie," Caroline hastened to assure her, interposing herself between Annie's recumbent form and the tall man. "He isn't really the earl, you know. He was just playing a nasty joke." Caroline turned to give him a brief but withering look and then turned back to her maid. "Do you feel altogether the thing?"

"Not the late earl?" Annie asked faintly, her eyes still riveted on the stranger.

"I am not," he declared gravely. "I have always been most punctual." Seeing the look of confusion that came over her face, he added kindly. "I am not a ghost, ma'am."

Caroline shot him a stern look before addressing her maid gently. "Are you feeling better, Annie?"

"Yes, I think so," Annie managed weakly. "Or, at least, I shall once we are home in dear Wiltshire again. I should have known better than to leave under such a bad omen as finding a glove turned inside out. I've been thinking," she continued hopefully as she raised herself to a sitting position on the couch. "Perhaps it would be best if we were to return to Wiltshire immediately. Your niece could come there."

"An excellent idea," Lord Devlon seconded her.

Caroline rounded on him, her hazel eyes snapping with smoldering anger. "I haven't the least interest in what you think, sir. I must own, I find it unhandsome of you in the extreme to play such an ill-conceived prank as to cause my maid to faint." Drawing herself up to her full height, which still left her some inches shorter than the earl, she finished with hauteur, "I fear I must ask you to leave this house at once."

Lord Devlon showed no sign that he meant to obey that command, or any other she might issue. Instead, he gave Caroline a look of pure insolence. "Indeed? And by what right do you give such an order?"

"My niece is the mistress of this house. I trust I speak in her best interest."

"How touching your concern for your niece is. May I say, I find it singularly remarkable that you arrive hard on the heels of your niece's husband's death to 'assist' her?"

"It is not, I think, unusual to comfort and offer aid to a bereaved widow," Caroline noted.

"In point of fact," he countered, "I do not believe the child is in need of anyone's help. She has done quite well on her own. Not only did she contrive to entrap my brother into marriage, but she was able to persuade him to have the great good sense to die promptly. Thus, she expected to have free rein of his money and property."

The fit of sputtering occasioned by that outrageous statement left Caroline devoid of speech for a good minute. Then the only words that came to her lips were an inane "You are the earl's brother?"

He gave a derisive smile that showed even white teeth in his darkly handsome face. "Permit me to introduce myself. I am Rye Bythestone, younger brother of Chester Bythestone. I have inherited the title and am now the eighth earl of Devlon. There is a bit more of a question concerning who has inherited the estate. I understand there was some sort of hackneyed will drawn up in which Chester bequeathed it to your niece. I shall shortly attend to that matter," he finished with an air of unconcern over such a a small detail.

"Oh," Caroline said after a shocked moment of staring speechlessly at the earl. Suddenly she was mindful that she was leaning slightly forward, her mouth parted in an expression of surprise and her eyes wide with shock. She hastily drew herself back and attempted to regain the reins of her shattered dignity. Brother? Caroline had not known Melissa's husband had a brother. But from the looks of the man before her he had a very troublesome one.

For his part, Lord Devlon was surveying the woman in front of him with condescending scorn. In her dusty rose pelerine, with short, disheveled auburn curls escaping from her démodé bonnet, she managed to look believably surprised. She was doubtless a very good actress, one who would have done credit to Drury Lane, but what utter nonsense to try to flummery him into thinking she had been unaware he existed.

Annie's words broke into the silent sparring. "Then you're not the dead earl?" she inquired, seeking final clarification.

"I am not."

"That's a blessing," she told him candidly. "I should dislike staying in a house with a dead man."

He gave a half smile. "I shouldn't think it will be necessary for you to stay, at any rate." Turning back to Caroline, he continued with frosty politeness, "It only remains for you to collect your niece and remove back to—" he gestured vaguely with a long, well-shaped hand, "wherever it is you come from."

Caroline looked at him coldly. His words implied he more than a little suspected she and Annie had crawled out from beneath some nearby rock. Indeed his whole attitude toward them seemed to be that of a bored man watching a pair of rather uninteresting ants make their way across a road.

"I am not here to 'collect' anyone, my lord," she informed him levelly. "My niece," she continued with a slightly harder inflection in her voice, "as you have just stated, owns this house and the land upon which you stand. I am unclear as to your reasons for being here, but I suggest you take yourself elsewhere where your presence will be more appreciated." And then she could not prevent herself from adding rudely, "If such a place exists."

The slow smile that lighted the earl's face had the effect of putting Caroline further out of countenance. She fervently wished she could think of something to say to give him a very proper set-down. But no such humbling words came to her mind, so she had to content herself with staring at him with freezing haughtiness.

"Miss Norton, you are fatigued from your journey. May I suggest you and your maid stay here for the night? In the morning when you are in a more rational frame of mind, I am persuaded you will see that I am entirely in the right of it. This is, after all, my family home. I certainly do not intend to stand by and watch it fall into the hands of . . ." He paused.

"Of what?" she challenged levelly.

He measured her with an assessing look. "Strangers," he finished blandly.

Caroline affected a sweeping look about the room, letting her eyes linger pointedly on the fading gold trim of the threadbare blue curtains, the aging dark blue velvet of the chairs and couches, and the worn carpet that had once been a fiery red and now made only a halfhearted attempt at dusky crimson.

"I can see that you are very solicitous about your family home," she told him with honeyed sarcasm.

"Therefore I understand why you are reluctant to lose such a showplace—nay, a palace. I bid you good day, my lord. As you have said, the matter of ownership is something that can be discussed at some later date. You have only to leave your direction with one of the servants with which the house abounds and, depend upon it, we shall be in close contact with you."

She gave him a smug smile. "Are you ready, Annie?" she asked, as her maid tottered to her feet and favored Lord Devlon with one final uncertain look. Caroline turned with a regal step and walked out of the room, followed closely by Annie, and continued out into the round hall without a backward look. She marched up the marble steps once again, determined to find a chambermaid, or footman, or someone in this ill-run household to show her to a room.

After peeping into three doorways, Caroline did discover a servant. She and Annie entered the room as he turned to face them. Laying aside the poker he had been using to stir the smoking fire, he moved toward them. He was a large man who walked with a rolling gait that put Caroline forcefully in mind of waves on a wind-tossed ocean. His beard and hair were as white as vellum: the only other prominent feature in his ruddy face was his dark, twinkling eyes.

"Demme, I wondered when you'd find yer way up 'ere," he greeted them unceremoniously.

"I beg your pardon?" Caroline said, affronted.

"Fool thing to run up and down the steps ever time what someone comes to the door. They'll find me if they really need somewhat," he continued.

"And so I tell that fool 'ousekeeper, er, Mrs. Whatever-'er-name is. And whom might ye be, missy?"

"I am the countess of Devlon's aunt," Caroline informed him. "I wish to be shown to my room, and then I want you to tell my niece I am here."

The old man watched her with wide eyes, coughed twice, and then nodded judiciously.

Satisfied with that response, Caroline folded her arms in front of her and waited for him to take some action. After the lapse of a minute or so with the old man still standing motionless before her, Caroline turned to Annie in exasperation. "Did he not hear me?"

"Perhaps," Annie ventured, her frightened eyes never leaving the man, "a witch has sent an evil spirit down the chimney and possessed his tongue. If we had a drop of witch's blood, that would keep it at bay from us. Although, what's to be done with *him,* I don't know."

The fat servant cast Annie a blighting look and snapped, "I can hear and I can talk. I jest don't know whether I should show ye to rooms."

"Not show us to our rooms! What nonsense is this?" Caroline cried.

"I ain't sure I should be 'llowing any of Miss Melissa's family into the 'ouse. That is to say, the new earl is arrivin' today and I don't doubt 'e'll throw the lot of ye out on yer ears. That kind of man 'e is," he explained apologetically.

"The earl does not own this house," Caroline grated out, stifling only with difficulty her urge to say considerably more about the earl that would be decidedly unflattering.

He lifted his wide shoulders in a shrug. "Mebbe, but I dasn't cross 'is lordship."

"Well, *I* have no qualms about it," Caroline replied in a frosty voice.

"I am certain *you* do not," a clipped voice spoke from the doorway. Lord Devlon ignored Caroline's furious look as he directed the servant, "Show the ladies rooms for the present, Frederick."

"As ye wish," Frederick capitulated gracelessly.

Caroline made no reply as she brushed past Lord Devlon out the door and followed the servant down the hall, fighting down her anger at the earl as she walked. She would not let him overset her, she resolved. Few men had and Lord Devlon was no better than any other *ton* man she had met.

And the earl was obviously *ton*. That much was evident from his clothes. He had discarded his greatcoat to reveal a blue waistcoat with brass buttons, brown leather breeches, and a deep, stiff cravat. The gloss of his black Hessian boots, complete with tassels, bespoke the air of a Corinthian. Well, Caroline didn't care if he was the prince regent himself—she would shortly give him to understand who was now in control of the house.

The old servant led the two women into a room covered with murky green wallpaper that had once depicted gay country scenes but now only managed to cling to the wall. An inelegant folding bed with trestle feet hugged a wall. Beside it was a chipped china bowl on a butterfly table with spindly legs.

Two banister-backed chairs of questionable age upholstered in rusty black completed the room's furniture. A lackluster rug covered the wooden floor.

Caroline stopped short. "My maid is not staying in this room," she declared firmly.

Frederick looked at her in surprise. " 'Tis for you."

The indignation his response aroused was not inconsiderable. "My good man, I wish to be shown to the very best room in the house! And immediately."

It was, apparently, the proper way to speak to Frederick, for he rolled out of the room and proceeded, albeit grumbling, to lead her down the hall to a stately suite.

There, past a comfortable sitting room, was a large bedroom that contained a tester bed richly adorned with posts displaying acanthus leaves carved in mellow walnut. The gold and purple curtains that framed the bed draped down to touch a vast Oriental rug of cream and deep orchid. Chairs covered in rich purple satin added further touches of elegance to the large room. And over the white-marble mantel, outlined in gold-leaf splendor, was a shield displaying the family coat of arms.

Caroline nodded her satisfaction. "This will do quite well. Now, kindly show my maid to her room."

Frederick gave an inaudible mutter and surged out of the room again. Annie trailed after him, stopping only long enough to advise Caroline to hang a rowan twig over her door to keep out witches.

Caroline absently nodded agreement as she looked around the room with the first traces of approval she had felt since her arrival. Everything she had encountered until now had been most curious. Where was Melissa? And what in the world had led Lord Devlon to come to his dead brother's house and act as if he owned it? And the servants were certainly not of the sort one expected to meet in an ordinary country house.

But, she decided as she stretched languorously, such matters would be shortly remedied. No doubt, an emergency had presented itself and called Melissa from the house on the very day Caroline was to arrive. All that would be explained later, she was sure. After a leisurely meal she and Melissa would have a pleasant coze. Then they could discuss the audacity of the new earl at coming to Hollowsby and acting so unforgivably rude.

fall out upon her spread. Everything she had in contemplation, till now, had been more vaguely. When was Mr Casaubon coming? She must go and ask him. Then she must come to the drawing-room again and see if everything would be in readiness. And there were notes — they were as ordinary as seen by

But, she decided at the last, being impatient, send Tantrippe and presently prepared had called to clear up. But, the houses on the new day the illusion came to arrive. All that would be expected later on, you sent. A nice a memory meal and she and plants a work have a pleasant basket. So prep could discuss the hundreds of the last at coming to Lowick copy and settling an interrupting time.

CHAPTER 4

Caroline felt another slight nudge on her shoulder. She shifted on the bed, moving away from the disturbing hand and snuggling back to the cozy, warm spot she had created for herself. Again the hand prodded her. This time she blinked her eyes open.

"Did I wake you up, Auntie Caro?", a small voice asked.

Instantly Caroline was fully awake. She sat up on the bed, facing the delicate, almost wraithlike vision that was her niece. Melissa's golden curls were nearly concealed under a black muslin cap that framed her small face. And her slender, girlish figure was engulfed in a heavy dress of black alpaca that fastened down the front to a plain skirt. The clothes looked like those of a much older woman.

"Melissa," Caroline said, rising to embrace her niece warmly. "I have been worried about you."

"I didn't mean for you to," Melissa assured her. "I didn't disturb you sooner because I thought you were sleeping. If I had known you were worrying about me I should have."

That speech, which would have sounded decidedly

cutting coming from anyone else, had a childlike forthrightness when delivered by Melissa. Caroline knew every word was spoken with truthful candor.

She gave a small laugh as she released Melissa. "I am found out. Perhaps I was not so very concerned as I might have been, but I *had* begun to wonder where you were. You were not here to greet me when I arrived," she chided gently.

Melissa's eyes, green and round in her pale oval face, grew even rounder at this knowledge. "But I did not know you were arriving today."

"Did you not receive my letter?"

"Of course, but it said you should be coming on the fifteenth and that isn't until . . ." Melissa paused. She set her small red mouth in a line, and her whole countenance became a moue of thoughtfulness as she tried to decide when the fifteenth might fall.

"It is today," Caroline informed her kindly.

"Oh!" Melissa's hand flew to her mouth. "I had forgotten the day of the month. I am most sorry, auntie. You aren't angry with me, are you?"

"Of course not," Caroline assured her. She wasn't: it was difficult to be angry with Melissa. The poor child was simple, but she would never intentionally hurt anyone, and Caroline had not the least wish to cause her any anxiety.

Melissa regarded her hesitantly and then, satisfied that her aunt really was not cross, cheerfully announced, "I have brought tea."

Gladdened by that news, Caroline abandoned her feeble attempts to straighten her rumpled gown and pat her hair down. She looked around the room and focused upon a tarnished silver tea service setting on a carved table by the mantel. "How very thoughtful of you, dear. I must own, I am near to famished."

Melissa smiled happily and confided, "I have brought all manner of sweets."

Better and better, Caroline thought, as they crossed the room together. She seated herself on a gilt and purple chair, settling back happily as she waited for Melissa to pour the tea into the wine-red Sevres cups.

The tea, lamentably, was cold; nevertheless Caroline continued to drink. She was quite hungry and this was not the time to complain about the servants, although she fully intended to approach the matter shortly. Just now, however, she had other things to discuss.

"Melissa, I wonder if you have given any thought as to how you intend to go on now that you are a widow." At her niece's blank stare Caroline continued in gentle explanation: "I mean, since the earl is dead, it is not altogether proper for you to live here alone. Technically, my dear, you are a dowager, but your young age prevents you from living alone with respectability. Do you understand?"

"Do you mean it will not be fitting for me to live without a companion?"

"Precisely." Caroline relaxed back in her chair.

"But isn't that why you have come?"

"I cannot stay indefinitely. Other people depend on me."

"Oh." Melissa looked crestfallen and uncertain.

"Don't worry, dear. It shouldn't be difficult for

you to find an older woman to live with you—one who is eminently acceptable to society and who can lend you countenance."

"Who?"

A very good question and one to which Caroline had already given a great deal of thought. Thus far, no names had occurred to her. After all, Georgiana had disgraced herself with all of polite society by the life she had lived. What acceptable matron would then consent to chaperon her daughter? Still, Melissa had inherited an estate and presumably some money from the earl. It was amazing how many doors that would open, especially from impoverished ladies who were no longer able to afford snobbery. But Caroline could not immediately think of any women of quality in such straits.

"I don't know," she admitted, "but I shall continue to think on it. Perhaps," she suggested hopefully, "your husband had some relation he mentioned to you—someone who would welcome you into her home?"

"I don't recall him ever speaking of such a person," Melissa said mournfully. "There was only his brother, and they were not on the best of terms."

Caroline sighed. She had not really expected there would be an aging aunt anxious to take Melissa in, but it had been worth a try.

"In fact," Melissa continued, looking off into the distance as she pursued her own train of thought, "Chester rarely even spoke of his brother. And that is rather a shame, because the new earl might have found a companion for me and let me stay on here if he and Chester had been on closer terms."

Caroline sat bolt upright in her chair, her teacup protesting with a vicious clatter. She set it down hastily and looked at Melissa intently. "What did you say?"

"I said he and his brother did not rub along well together."

"Yes," Caroline agreed impatiently, "but what did you say about his brother letting you stay here?"

"Oh," Melissa said uncertainly, crossing her hands in her lap in agitation. "Have you not met him? I thought—from his words to me earlier—that he had already given you to understand he wishes us out of the house immediately. He means to have the marriage nullified if we try to stay," she added absently.

As Caroline's lips worked soundlessly, Melissa elucidated, "He wants us all out—you and I and your maid and my dog Clover and—"

"Melissa, what utter nonsense! Of course he can make no such demands."

"Well," her niece agreed meekly, "I did think perhaps he might allow Clover to stay, as it is a very large house, and a dog goes on so much better in a big place than he would in a small one. And I am certain I shall have to live somewhere much smaller if I lose Chester's house and his money in the bargain."

"Clover shall certainly stay!" Caroline intoned angrily, standing to pace toward the window and look out at the emerald-green lawns. "The very nerve of the man to bully this poor child!"

"I'm ever so glad of that," Melissa declared thankfully. "Then I shall not mind having to make my own living if Clover is taken care of. And I shall be able to bear losing all this. Although," she admitted with a trace of longing in her voice, "I do like it here."

"Melissa," Caroline stormed, turning from the window and pacing to the mantel in agitation, "you do not understand in the least. No man, woman, child, or dog is forced to leave Hollowsby unless *you* give the command for them to do so."

"But the new earl said—"

"And the more so because *he* said it!" Caroline expostulated.

"But he . . ." Melissa pursued feebly.

"I have not the least interest in his ravings," Caroline snapped. At the sight of the glistening tears that sprang into Melissa's eyes, she hastened to her niece's side and drew her into a comforting embrace. "I'm not angry with you, dear. You simply must understand that the man has no say over your life. Doubtless he is at *Point-non plus* and thinks to regain his fortune by trying to persuade you he controls this estate. I assure you he does not, and he shall shortly see that you do not intend to give in to his bullying. Then he will move on, looking for some other poor, defenseless woman from whom to steal a fortune, I don't doubt."

Melissa looked perplexed. "But Chester always said his brother was very well to pass, so I can't think he needs the money. Today he seemed almost to dislike me. I cannot think why, as he had never met me before. And I took great care to be amiable to him, and I *did* apologize profusely for dropping hot wax on his hands, as well as for burning the very smallest of holes in his lawn shirt, but everyone drops a candle now and again, do they not? And I—"

Caroline stemmed this flow of words by saying quickly, "Perhaps it is not the money he desires. But let us not discuss his lordship just now. First we should decide where you wish to live. There are problems here, of course. For one thing, the deplorable condition of the house. Then there is the matter of the servants—what few there are of them. And their incompetence! Imagine, being sent cold tea and stale scones!"

"I'm sorry," Melissa offered swiftly, her green eyes penitent. "I thought I had got the tea quite hot enough, but I am not so very used to cooking and—"

"*You* made the tea?" Caroline interrupted in disbelief.

"Yes, and I'm dreadfully sorry if it displeases you. I can take it back," she offered, rising, "and try to get it hotter, although I am not altogether certain how—"

Caroline inhaled a deep breath of air and strove to remain calm. "Sit down, Melissa." She waited until her niece obeyed. "Now then, how comes it that you should be the one to make the tea?"

"Oh," Melissa explained simply, "the servants began to resign shortly after Chester's death. Well, actually, my maid ran off with the local blacksmith first. Then the butler left with the upstairs maid.

They were brother and sister, you understand." She stopped to think and then added, "At least they *said* they were when they left together, but I had not known it before then. Do you suppose they were?"

"I wouldn't know."

"Yes, well, now only a few servants remain. And they're dreadfully busy trying to do everything, so I decided to make my own tea. Only, as you can see, I'm not very good at it. I daresay, I shall improve with practice. Don't you think?"

"No," Caroline cried, and moderated her tone at her niece's disappointed look. "I think that new servants need to be employed. Do you wish to continue to live here?"

At Melissa's mute nod Caroline continued: "Then, I shall write to an agency in London to find replacements for the vacant positions. In the meantime we must also initiate plans to go to London ourselves to begin selection of materials and furniture." Caroline paused. "New furniture is necessary. Once the house is refurbished you can decide whether you wish to maintain Hollowsby merely as your country home and set up another establishment in London or whether you want to live here year-round. Of course, it would be best to remain here until your year of mourning is up."

Melissa nodded in wide-eyed fascination before taking a final swallow of her tea. "I'm so glad you've come, Auntie Caro. I know you will have everything right as a trivet in no time."

"I intend to," Caroline assured her with a smile as she rose. She patted her niece's hand affectionately.

"And now, if you could find a servant to have my trunk brought up, I shall change into something suitable for dinner."

Melissa gave a respectful nod and walked from the room, looking content in the knowledge that someone had arrived to take over the worrisome burden of dealing with servants and ordering the household.

For her part Caroline settled down to await the arrival of her trunk with a glow of satisfaction. She would shortly infuse some badly needed organization into Hollowsby. It was apparent no one had seen to the house for years. Poor Melissa did not have the first notion how to manage a house of this size. Caroline did not doubt that the land suffered from the same lack of attention. But she would deal with that later, she resolved, as the door opened and Frederick ambled in, plopped her trunk in the spot she indicated at the foot of the bed, and left again.

Caroline opened it and began to sort through her clothes, looking for just the right gown for this evening. She wanted something entirely elegant, to show the remaining servants that things were going to be different around the house from now on. And, if the impertinent Lord Devlon was still in residence, she wanted him to see that she was a woman of fashion.

She held several gowns up in front of her before settling on a pea-green satin petticoat with a white net drapery over it. It had an oval, off-shoulder décolletage edged with ecru frilling. A high waistline draped gracefully to a double row of flounces decorated with the selfsame frilling.

Surveying herself in the cheval glass, Caroline

noted approvingly that the gown showed her bosom to advantage without being shockingly low. The servants would see this was not the gown of a woman who would tolerate the likes of cold tea. And, what was more, the tasteful string of matching pearls and diamond-and-pearl earrings she selected would convince the new earl that he was dealing with a wealthy woman of the world.

Yes, Caroline decided with confidence, she would make brief work of Lord Devlon and the servants. Then she and Melissa could get about their real concern—that of refurbishing the house to its former glory. Lord, it would be impossible to sell it in this condition, even if Melissa wished to. But when they had finished, it would be a masterpiece where her niece could live comfortably if she chose to stay. Poor lamb, Caroline thought, as she considered how miserable Melissa must have been before her arrival. Well, she would take care of her, she vowed with a surge of protectiveness. At least she could make the house habitable for her.

Of course, such an undertaking would take long months to complete. That realization gave Caroline a moment's pause and she stopped in the act of fastening on an earring. Well, and what if it did? She couldn't desert Melissa until it was finished, so she would simply stay. Besides, she rather thought she would enjoy the project. Already she could envision the dowdy room Lord Devlon had carried Annie into cleared of its heavy antiques and refurbished with cardinal red drapes falling in crisp lines to replace the blue rags that now hung there. And tasteful

Georgian furniture with fine linen coverings in mint or tan would be a pleasant change from the dark velvet.

Caroline was so wound up in her thoughts that she didn't even think to call Annie to assist her. She was giving her bronze curls—a few of which framed her face becomingly before being drawn into a little cluster on the crown of her head—a final pat before descending to the drawing room to await dinner. There she and Melissa could discuss plans for the house. More and more ideas for it were occurring to Caroline as she stepped out into the hall. With a dainty wrinkle of her nose, she stopped to look at the hunting scenes in somber browns and bleary reds that hung on the walls. They were surrounded by heavy busts on oversized pedestals. All these would definitely go—she made a mental note as she continued the length of the hall.

She walked down the marble staircase and proceeded toward the east wing to the drawing room Melissa had given her directions to. Her niece was not in sight as she stepped into the maroon-colored room, but over by the fireplace, looking relaxed and irritatingly comfortable, was the earl. He rose as she came into the room, but his face never lost its bored look, even as he nodded to her.

Caroline had been about to seat herself in a chair by the window, but instead she marched to the fireplace. In one graceful movement, she seated herself in a chocolate-brown, overstuffed chair opposite the earl and joined him in looking at the fireplace.

"Good evening," he said coldly as he reseated himself.

She deigned to bestow a haughty look at him, nodded and turned back toward the smoldering fire in the grate as if its charred and smoking embers were a subject of intense fascination.

He studied her laconically. A bit more handsome than he had thought earlier, he concluded, but much too independent and headstrong. Not that he had any interest in her anyway. He had not reached the age of two and thirty unwed by succumbing to the charms of every passably attractive chit. And were he looking about for a wife, which he certainly was not, this one would not have appealed to him. In point of fact, his only interest in her lay in ridding himself of her and her simpleminded niece.

Putting his thoughts into their simplest form, he asked bluntly, "When are you leaving?"

"I beg your pardon?" Her words were laden with the weight of icicles and her eyes were equally cold as she looked from the fire to the earl.

"I asked when you and your niece would be removing from my family home," he repeated, unperturbed.

"We have no such plans, my lord." Her words were curt and succinct.

Lord Devlon ran an impatient hand through his dark hair. Miss Norton was a troublesome piece to be sure, but he had best humor her for the present. It was obvious she was the one he would have to deal with. His brother's widow was entirely empty-headed. "I am sorry if my words have offended," he began rationally. "But you must know my family has been in this house since 1690."

"Indeed," was her stony reply.

"Some of them," he admitted with a small smile, "are dead now."

No answering smile relaxed her face to indicate his little bit of humor had been appreciated, or even recognized. Instead she said very somberly, "You are to be consoled on their loss. I feel quite close to all of the members of your venerable family. Only this afternoon I dined on tea and scones that were clearly left from your great-grandfather's tea in the 1700s."

It was the earl's turn to ignore her thrust. Instead he slowly placed his long legs out before him and looked speculatively at the tasseled tops of his boots. "If you do not leave I shall have the marriage set aside. That would create quite a scandal—something I think neither of us wishes. After all, you must own it is highly unlikely the marriage was legal. Your niece was only a child. Therefore," he concluded logically, "I suggest you simply depart and the whole matter will die quietly.

"The only way I shall leave this house with you in residence is to be carried dead out the door," she told him unencouragingly.

He gave a dispassionate shrug. "Difficult, but not impossible."

Caroline threw him a repressive look and rose to walk to the window. "This house bids fair to falling down. If you were so mightily interested in it, how has that come about?" Without pausing for him to reply, she continued, "Or is it only since my niece has inherited it that it has become your ruling passion?"

He eyed her thoughtfully. "It is not my 'ruling passion' as you so quaintly phrase it. I have other, more interesting passions, Miss Norton. It is, however, my family home."

"*Was* your family home," she intervened belligerently.

Lord Devlon continued undaunted. "As I was saying, I did not own it before and when I paid my last visit to my brother and attempted to discuss the shocking state it had fallen into, he ordered me from the house. Blatant signs of inhospitality, wouldn't you say?"

"Richly deserved, I don't doubt," Caroline noted.

"But hardly the act of a gentleman."

"I'm sure your ideas on that head are very fine," she rejoined.

He bowed politely. "I thank you for the compliment. I am persuaded you are an excellent judge."

CHAPTER 5

The earl looked around the dining room with interest. The rectangular room had long windows swathed in russet drapes that dulled all traces of the sun, even at midday. The flickering candles in ornate candelabra revealed high-backed Tudor chairs covered with the same russet damask. They were lined around a long table that was set with heavy pieces of Limoges china. An epergne of silver in the process of turning black, provided the centerpiece.

The room was, he concluded, the same as it had been when he was a boy, only somewhat the worse for wear. He glanced down at the two women who sat at the other end of the table, separated from him by a half dozen chairs. With a wry smile he considered that the assembled parties resembled opposing camps at a council of war.

"The roads were deplorable," Caroline began cordially. Whatever her personal feelings toward the earl might be, she was too much of a lady to brawl with him at the dining room table, she thought virtuously.

"It was," he returned, unhampered by her resolutions, "wholly unnecessary for you to have come at all. You could have saved yourself the unpleasantness of the roads. I fear you shall not have sufficient time to rest before you are obliged to leave again." He spoke in the matter-of-fact tones of one stating a truth that was lamentable but couldn't be helped.

Caroline gave him a sharp look but answered placidly, "My niece and I shall not be leaving, my lord. I think you must be a bit unclear about the contents of your late brother's will. It states, I believe, that Hollowsby becomes his wife's upon his death."

The earl tasted a bite of the first course. It was a decidedly pasty gravy soup that was entirely in keeping with what he had seen of the housekeeping thus far. Lord, it was obvious this child didn't know the first thing about managing a household.

He ignored Caroline's words while pursuing his own line of thought. "You are not married, Miss Norton?"

"No, I am not," she replied, her face betraying confusion at his unexpected question.

"You have never been married?" he probed, laying aside his spoon as he abandoned the attempt to eat his unappetizing course.

"No, I have not."

"I see," he replied and addressed himself once again to the meal as a servant removed the sticky soup and replaced it with a gray-looking fish.

"I cannot understand what it is that you see, my lord," she noted testily. "My marriage, or lack of it, has nothing to say to the matter of my niece's inheritance."

"No," he acknowledged. "However, I find it singularly interesting that you should descend on my house so shortly after the death of my brother. I assume you had never met him."

"No, I had not had the honor," she replied with stiff dignity.

"Pity."

"I fail to see what all these cryptic remarks have to say to my niece's rightful claim to Hollowsby. And," she added defiantly, "I did not 'descend' on this house. Mice and other unwanted creatures, I believe, do that. Certainly the aunt of an owner does not."

Lord Devlon's look clearly implied he thought Caroline fell neatly into the category of unwanted creatures, but he did not address that matter. "The questions, Miss Norton," he returned, "reveal to me quite plainly what I essentially already knew. You and—" he flicked a bored glance at Melissa, who sat white-faced and motionless listening to the words being flung across the table, "Miss Courtney appear to me to be a set of adventuresses, not to say, fortune hunters. As the young lady," again a slight inclination of his dark head toward Melissa, "is underage, I presume you raced here to try to make her outrageous claim to Hollowsby stick."

That should send them very nicely to grass, he thought with satisfaction. Once it became obvious he meant to dispense with senseless commonplaces and deal with them directly, they would leave soon enough. The child had been too young to have made a legal marriage without the consent of a parent.

Since no parent was in evidence, only this grasping aunt, he felt certain that consent had never been given. He would make short work of overturning this preposterous will.

Caroline squeezed Melissa's hand reassuringly under the table, took a sip of water, patted her lips with the yellowing linen napkin and smiled with gracious condescension. "Have you tried the fish? I must own I find it rather unappealing. It affects me the way some people do," she murmured with a sweet smile.

Lord Devlon continued brittlely. "Make no mistake, Miss Norton; I shall not fail in ridding my family home of the pair of you." He noted with satisfaction that Melissa paled visibly at his words. Perhaps it wouldn't be so troublesome to unseat them after all. His brother's wife, a mere scrap of a chit dressed in a ridiculously ancient black gown, appeared manageable enough. But the aunt might prove tenacious. "Do I make myself clear?" he asked with unveiled contempt.

"I had wondered when your veneer of excessively charming amiability would wear off," Caroline said pleasantly. "I did not think your health would permit you to hold your spleen in any longer."

"I am touched by your solicitude for my health."

The arrival of a tottering old man in fading blue livery bearing a fricassee of rabbit necessitated a temporary stifling of hostilities. But Caroline could see that the earl's eyes, cold and hard, still carried the lash of his pent-up anger.

Melissa ventured into the menacing silence with a

dubious look from her aunt to Lord Devlon. "I think it has been lovely weather and I don't doubt it will continue to be so. My dog Clover—he's such a nice dog—and I went for a walk just this afternoon. It was ever so lovely. The cliffs down by the sea are especially pretty." She smiled at the other two diners.

Caroline, taking pity on Melissa's pathetic attempt to steer the conversation toward more pleasant channels, smiled kindly at her. "I'm persuaded they are, dear."

"Would you like to see them sometime?"

"Indeed, I would."

The talk between Caroline and her niece continued in an innocuous vein. The earl did not join the conversation. For Caroline the dinner was hauntingly reminiscent of the meals she had endured from the time she was twelve until she left her home to go to London for her presentation. She and Georgiana had sat at one end of the table, very like she and Melissa did now, while their father presided over the other end. In fact, Caroline considered as Melissa chattered on about her dog, there was much in the cold earl that reminded her of her father. Robert Norton had been a cynical man ever since she could remember, although he may have been different before their mother died. At any rate, until his own death four years ago he had never showed by word or deed that he cared in the least for his daughters.

Caroline had often wondered if the memory of their father accounted for why Georgiana never stayed with one man long and why she herself studiously avoided any man who showed an interest in her. After all, she had enough money to be comfortable so why should she willingly tie herself to a man who would not make her happy? Caroline was not so lost to romantic thoughts that she did not now and again think of a perfect man riding into her life whom she would fall madly in love with. If that should happen she would marry him gladly; it was not that she had anything against matrimony, it was just that she was wary of men.

Trevina had once accused her of not giving any man a chance but Caroline did not believe that was true. She could take a man's measure very quickly and she could always tell immediately that they would not suit. Besides, Trevina was inclined to see all men as better than they really were. Why, she would probably even be finding good things to say about Lord Devlon and he was even colder and harsher than her father had been. Some poor woman had been saved a dismal fate by the fact Lord Devlon had never married. He must be all of three and thirty so it was not likely that he would now.

At the other end of the table, the earl was unaware of Caroline's thoughts about him. His mind was thoroughly occupied with deciding what measures he must take to persuade this underaged widow and her greedy aunt to leave Hollowsby. Although he was certain the child had no legal claim to the estate, he didn't wish to embarrass his family name by publically disputing her right to it. No, the best course, he resolved wearily, was to simply buy the chits off.

"Could I have a few words with you ladies in the

study?" he asked as the meal concluded. "Concerning the estate," he added as he saw the older woman hesitate.

"You go, Auntie Caro," Melissa said quickly. "I must see to Clover. He becomes so bored and longs for company."

"But Melissa, this is something for which you really should be present," Caroline objected.

The younger woman turned pleading eyes to her aunt that bespoke clearly her wish to escape the earl's presence as quickly as possible. Caroline softened in the face of Melissa's appeal. "Very well," she acquiesced.

Moments later Caroline was seated in the study, a large square room whose walls were lined with volumes of leather-bound books. The center of the room was dominated by a large oak desk and behind it was a fireplace of black marble. Altogether it was a dark, authoritative-looking room. The man in the portrait over the fireplace, who glared down on Caroline with a disconcerting resemblance to the earl, only made it more so.

She stared at Lord Devlon—the present one—across the wide desk and wondered how it had come to pass that she was seated in the visitor's chair like some housemaid applying for a position, while he sat behind the desk, looking like the lord of the manor.

"Now then," Lord Devlon began with abrupt authority, "I think you and I shall be able to deal together very well once we understand each other. As I mentioned, I intend to have the marriage nullified if you persist in your claims. But surely there is a better way. Why not simply have my estate signed back to me and I will give your niece a generous settlement? Miss Courtney, being under legal age, as well as a bit of a—" He broke off and regarded the woman across from him hesitantly. "Let us be honest, Miss Norton. The child is a dull wit. She need not be bothered except to sign the necessary papers. I see it is you I shall have to deal with."

Caroline bristled at his description of Melissa. How dare he talk of her niece that way! "I fail to see how you consider this your estate."

He proceeded with forbearing amiability. "I think it would be to the point if I described something of the family background so that you will understand how matters came to this point. Once you see that," and your palm is weighted with the proper amount of money, he added silently, "I don't doubt you will see the wisdom of leaving."

"My brother, Miss Norton, was ever a wastrel. After my father's death he pursued a life of aimless enjoyment. He gamed, hunted, and—how shall I put this delicately enough?—pursued a certain type of woman."

The earl paused to gauge Caroline's reaction, but she only stared at him silently. "At any rate," he continued, "it was a selfish life that served little purpose beyond the pursuit of his own pleasures. He also," Lord Devlon continued with a harder inflection in his voice, "let the house fall near to pieces and engaged in all manner of ungentlemanly pursuits. Finally, he committed the most indiscreet of all offenses: He married a child of no breeding, and, quite obviously, no character."

Caroline's hot words of protest were stilled by his upflung hand. "And there were even more inexcusable actions to boot. It appears that Chester not only leg-shackled himself to the child..." he rose to pace the book-lined room in agitation, clasping his hands behind him, "but he also had the total lack of sense to make up some sort of will leaving my family estate to the addlepated girl." He turned to glare at Caroline as if demanding an explanation for his brother's actions.

She could be silent no longer. "You insult my niece, my lord!"

His eyes met her flashing eyes coolly. He had dealt with money-mad women before. In fact, with her rather delicate looks she reminded him of a certain lightskirt he had once had in keeping who was constantly performing such histrionics. Miss Norton's look of outraged dignity carried not the least weight with him.

"Don't toy with me, ma'am. You'll soon find yourself outmaneuvered." His voice was unforged steel. "If you choose not to meet my generous offer, I shall have no alternative but to have the marriage voided and turn both of you out. Then you can look about for some other person to fasten yourself upon." He returned to his perambulation.

"Your thoughts reflect mine exactly, only the names are changed. *You* are the person looking for an innocent to feed upon."

"How very ghoulish, Miss Norton. I see you suffer

from the same overactive imagination that afflicts your maid." Lord Devlon glared down at the woman seated on the other side of the desk. It was ironic, he thought, that she could manage to look so innocent and dainty when she was embroiled in a most unsavory plot. In fact, with her hazel eyes wide and sparkling with anger and her small red mouth in a firm line, Miss Norton looked damnably attractive. She had that way ladies possess of always being able to look the injured party. At least he could be thankful she had not dissolved into tears as so many women of his acquaintance would have done. But that was apparently an artifice she eschewed. He must be thankful for small favors.

While Caroline gazed unwaveringly at the earl thoughts were running rapidly through her mind. The first was that she meant to protect her niece from this man at all costs. When her mother had died, there had been no one to perform that function for her and Georgiana. They had been forced to suffer the brunt of their father's ill temper alone. Not that he had ever physically misused them, for he had not. But there were more subtle ways to make a child feel miserable, and the most effective one was to make them feel unwanted. That was what the earl was doing to Melissa. Already the poor girl wished to escape the house to be away from this fierce man. Well, he wouldn't bully them into leaving if Caroline had anything to say about it. If she did not look after her niece's interest, then who would?

She almost jumped when he said, "I repeat, how much money do you want?"

Caroline rose and walked to the door. Turning, she said proudly, "Were you to offer my niece all the riches of China in return for this tumbledown remnant of a mansion, I would advise her not to sell to *you*."

"Take that, my fine lord," she muttered under her breath as she closed the door with a firm hand and marched down the hallway and up the stairs to her room.

Inside it, however, she found Annie waiting for her, and her maid's words did nothing to soothe her already ruffled temper.

"I dislike this house and all about it," Annie greeted her with a foreboding look.

"Why is that?" Caroline asked with halfhearted interest as she walked to the center of the purple room and turned to allow Annie to help her from her gown.

"For one thing, the food is revolting! I cannot recall ever being served anything as terrible before. Well," she amended conscientiously, "Parson Windrift was a bit of a clutch-fist, and many's the time I thought I should starve there. I don't doubt I should have, too, but that I discovered where he hid the key to the larder."

Caroline nodded wearily but she was scarcely listening. It had been a long day and she was tired. She was pulling her nightclothes from the highboy when a scratching at the door drew both women's attention. "Come in," Caroline called.

Melissa entered and stood in the doorway. "I

thought you might wish to meet Clover before bedtime."

At the sound of his name an animal that could best be described as half wolf and half horse bounded into the room, looked ferociously about, and gave an ear-shattering bark. Annie and Caroline both scrambled backward away from the sharp-toothed, hard-eyed creature with inky-black hair.

From atop her perch on the bed Annie shrieked and begged to be saved while Caroline tried to appear calm in the face of the vicious-looking dog. Her hands reached outward for the poker as she took quick steps backward toward the fireplace.

Melissa looked from the maid to her aunt. "Do you not like dogs?" she asked innocently.

Clover's fearsome growl pervaded the room like the angry call of a raging mountain lion.

"It's not precisely that," Caroline assured her in a shaking voice as her hands closed thankfully over the cold steel of the poker. "It is merely that I did not expect a house dog to be of such size."

She moved another step backward until she was against the wall. Her hands nervously fingered the poker, prepared to swing if necessity dictated it.

"He's a wonderful house dog," Melissa extolled. "It is only that he is not used to sharing his room, and he does not know you."

"His room!" Caroline cried.

"I should give it to him if I were you, ma'am," Annie advised hastily.

"Well, yes, it is his room," Melissa admitted,

dropping down on her knees to take the dog's head in an affectionate embrace. "See how very sweet he can be."

"His room," Caroline repeated dumbfounded.

"Yes. Chester was very fond of Clover and directed that he have the very best room in the house. I cannot think why Frederick gave you this room. He knows Clover cannot abide sharing his bed with anyone."

"Share a bed with that animal! I should think not," Caroline exclaimed. "Why was I put in this room if—" she broke off as she recalled her command to Frederick to show her to the best room in the house. "Wait until I get my hands on that rascal," she muttered.

"What?" Melissa asked.

"Nothing." That was something that would wait until later. Right now it was far more to the point to remove this loathsome beast from her room.

It was an idea that proved easier in the making than it did in the execution. Annie bailed off the far side of the bed screaming as Clover jumped up onto it. He looked around the room with the air of a king surveying a dirty mob of unruly peasants and gave one final masterful snarl before stretching out the length of the bed and closing his eyes.

"Do you wish me to try to rouse him?" Melissa asked hesitantly. "He isn't always so very agreeable when he is awakened."

"No," Caroline replied swiftly. "Don't bother him. I shall find another chamber. I am certain a house this large abounds with them. Perhaps I could be shown to the second best chamber."

"The earl is sleeping there. Of course we could ask him to move to my chamber and you could have his and then I—"

"It doesn't signify," Caroline interrupted, acknowledging defeat. "In the morning you and I can sit down and address the matter of sleeping arrangements. For the present I only want a room that is not occupied by a dog or a man with the manners of one. I trust there is still a bed to be had in the house."

"Of course," Melissa assured her cheerfully.

Caroline stopped only long enough to pick up her nightclothes, being careful not to turn her back on the huge black animal occupying what had been her bed until just minutes ago.

She walked out the door and followed Melissa down the hall while Annie scurried after them. Melissa enumerated Clover's many virtues as Annie made inarticulate sentences about a dog who had once eaten all the members of a large family because they had foolishly planted parsley near the house. Everyone, she mumbled, knew that was very bad luck.

Caroline continued down the hall wordlessly, wondering how it happened that she had spent a jolting day making the journey from Wiltshire to arrive at a house that was in a decidedly ramshackle condition. On top of that she had been treated to a most ungentlemanly speech by a man who had no claim to this house. And furthermore, she had been served food that was well nigh inedible, and she was now being turned out of her room by a creature that walked on four legs and had the distinct influence—and not so very far back in this particular creature's lineage, she suspected—of a wolf. It was an inauspicious beginning to her visit, to be sure.

CHAPTER 6

"Clover," Melissa informed Caroline as her aunt doubtfully eyed the greenish-yellow buttered eggs before her, "misses Chester dreadfully. Don't you, Clover?" Melissa asked, reaching down to give the dog an affectionate pat on the head where he sat curled up beneath her chair in the breakfast parlor.

Clover growled his bereavement and then returned to noisy snoring—a sound which Caroline found an extreme source of annoyance. She put a biteful of the unappetizing eggs into her mouth and attempted to eat them.

"He is ever such a smart dog," Melissa pursued in an effort to spark some kindly emotion in her aunt's breast for the sleeping animal.

"I am certain he is," Caroline replied noncommittally. Her full attention at the moment was centered on the eggs in her mouth. Was it possible a piece of rubber could have been put on her plate by mistake? It was scarcely conceivable that hen's eggs could be this resistant to chewing.

The sound of heavy bootsteps thudding into the room caused both women to glance up. The earl, looking well turned out in a single-breasted claret morning coat, dowlas trousers, and a Barrel knot cravat tied neatly at his neck, helped himself to several dishes from the sideboard before seating himself in a chair at the small rectangular table. After the briefest of acknowledgments he turned his full attention to his meal.

Lord Devlon was startled out of his complacent examination of his breakfast by the resounding explosion of a noise very nearby.

"Good God!" He turned startled eyes around the room before they came to rest on the recumbent form of Clover beneath Melissa's chair. The dog snarled meaningfully and subjected the newcomer to an unfriendly scrutiny.

"What is that creature doing here?" the earl asked. A touch of repugnance laced his voice.

"It's my dog," Melissa explained. "His name is Clover and he's ever so smart. He can sit up and—"

"I am aware it is a dog," he told her in quelling accents. "What I wish to know is what it is doing in the breakfast room."

"He always eats here. Chester was very fond of him. He even named him after his favorite grass. And he always liked Clover to eat with us. Chester often fed him scraps from the table," she suggested helpfully, looking to see if the earl wished to do likewise. "You could feed him if you like," she said when Lord Devlon ignored her broad hint.

"Thank you, but I may have need of my hand at some later date, and I do not wish to have it severed at the wrist by that wolf. Get it out of here," he finished curtly.

Melissa, shocked at hearing Clover dismissed in such a cavalier manner, persevered in the teeth of rejection. "Oh, he wouldn't bite you, my lord. He's ever so gentle. Only pet him and you will see that he really is quite loving."

"Get him out," the earl enunciated in crisp, hard words.

Melissa rose slowly and obeyed, leading a sulking Clover from the room with quiet assurances that he and the new earl would soon become quite fond of each other. "Don't worry, Clover," she prattled, "he didn't mean to hurt your feelings...." Her voice died away as she trailed off down the hall with Clover in tow.

Caroline, torn between relief at seeing the last of the dog and chagrin that Lord Devlon had been the one to effect his removal, laid her fork down with a sharp clatter. "I shall excuse myself," she informed him haughtily, preparing to rise.

He pushed his plate away with a muttered curse and looked at her with a dark scowl. "Is there nothing fit to eat in the whole of the house?"

"I am not the cook!" she exclaimed indignantly. How dare he speak to her in such a way?

"If any of us is to escape starvation, perhaps you should master the art, Miss Norton. At least then your presence here would serve some useful purpose."

"Were I to undertake such a task, I would relish serving my first efforts to you, my lord," she retorted.

He continued, heedless of her words. "The state of this household is by everything considered inexcusable. This morning I even wrote my name in the dust on a table."

"Could you not find any paper?" she asked with feigned innocence.

Lord Devlon ran his hand through his hair. There was nothing to be served by antagonizing this woman. It would be far better if he were to stifle his feelings toward her and her niece until some arrangement could be made to rid them from his home. In a conciliatory tone, he said, "I beg your pardon, Miss Norton. I fear I am not at my best in the morning."

Caroline regarded him suspiciously. His eyes were two deep blue pools; it was impossible to read anything in them. But he did sound repentant. "Of course, my lord," she said mildly. She hadn't seen him yet when he was at his best but she forbore to comment on that. Far better that he be in an amiable mood than the dark one she had seen yesterday. It would certainly make Melissa feel a good deal more comfortable.

"I fear the house is in a sad state of disrepair," Lord Devlon said ruefully as he looked about the room.

"It does seem to require a bit of paint here and there," Caroline rejoined politely. It was in need of a good deal more than that, but there was no reason to state the obvious.

"I thought I would ride about the estate a bit later and see how the tenants' cottages have fared. Chester always took a great interest in his tenants, so I trust their homes have not suffered from the same lack of repairs."

"Let us hope they have not." She took a sip of her hot chocolate and surreptitiously studied the earl over the rim of her cup. He was impeccably and expensively attired in a claret waistcoat and white breeches.

Caroline had puzzled over the earl last night, trying to decide whether she had met him in any London drawing room during her come-out. She did not recall his face. Of course, she had been introduced to a good many men, but she thought she would remember the earl. With his tall, athletic physique and darkly attractive face, he was not a man one would forget.

If he was *ton*, and she was certain he was, then she could only assume he moved in higher circles than she had. Although Mrs. Trimen, the woman who had presented her, was of a moderately wealthy family, it was not an old one. Mrs. Trimen had been admitted to a good many houses of fashionable repute, but she had not been invited to those of the first respectability. Were those the salons Lord Devlon frequented? It was a lowering thought to consider that he was socially above her touch. Caroline set her cup down and studied it absently. She would certainly give him no hint she had concluded that he was. After all, the question here was not one's social standing; it was a legal matter of inheritance.

"Where is your niece's father?" Lord Devlon asked cautiously. If he could only sort through this tangle of females and talk to a man surely things would go easier. The chit's father would be willing to deal with him and make a simple cash settlement, he was certain. Then the whole ugly business would be concluded.

"Melissa's father is deceased, my lord," Caroline replied.

"I see." Damn, it was just his luck. Well, if there was only one parent left then he would have to deal with the child's mother. "And her mother?" he ventured carefully.

"She is abroad," Caroline replied casually. She rose with a smile. There were things she did not wish to explain: where Georgiana was and whom she was living with figured chief among those. Let Lord Devlon find his own sources of information. "If you will excuse me," she said courteously. "I wish to take a turn about the garden."

"Of course." He rose as she left.

In the garden Caroline sat down on a bench and considered what was to be done next. Although she realized Melissa owned the house, Lord Devlon had asked questions that made it clear he meant to pursue his course of taking it from her. He was going to uncover some things about their family that Caroline wished he would not discover.

She was so absorbed in her brown study that she did not hear Melissa approach a short time later. Indeed it was only when her niece asked, "Is there something wrong with the flowers, Auntie Caro?" that Caroline became aware she had company.

"No, they are delightful."

Melissa brightened. "I'm so glad you like them.

Wildflowers are the only things Frederick has been able to grow, although the gardener, the one who resigned, had excessively good luck with camellias. But I thought perhaps you didn't like wildflowers because you were giving them a dreadfully sour look."

Caroline smiled at her niece's words. There was no need to let the child know her thoughts. Patting the seat beside her, she said, "Sit down, dear. Did you want something?"

"Oh, yes, I did," Melissa replied, suddenly mindful she had not come to discuss the vegetation. "Could we go into town?" I have not been since Chester's death, but I think I should obtain some different mourning clothes." She gestured toward her aging dress with a cheery smile. "This is serviceable for here, but if we need to travel it is not so very fashionable. I found these clothes in a trunk in the attic," she explained.

"You are perfectly right, dear. Those clothes are beyond the pale." Rags would have been a more appropriate word to describe Melissa's attire, but Caroline didn't want to hurt her feelings. "Only let me change my clothes and I will be ready to accompany you."

Half an hour later Caroline was clad in a new cranberry-colored muslin gown with white ribbons adorning the scalloped neckline. Over her arm she carried a sable brown pelerine as she descended the steps with Annie.

Stepping outside, she noted appreciatively that the sun shone brightly. Only a few white fluffs of clouds flirted with it, dancing across it now and again to block its bright rays.

"It's a lovely day," Melissa remarked.

"Yes," Caroline agreed as she gazed off toward Golden Gap. She was glad for the chance to be away from the house for a time, and she didn't doubt an outing with Melissa would prove a pleasant enough afternoon.

The horses set off at a brisk pace on a road of extraordinary narrowness, steep in ascent and descent. The carriage inched up to the crest of each hill with steady determination before rolling down the other side at a speed that made Caroline's stomach turn over. Finally and none too soon, Caroline thought as she gingerly removed her clenched fists from atop her lap, the road turned inland and wound across gorse-covered commons and a scattering of woodland. Just as they emerged from a copse, Caroline spied the town below.

Actually the name "town" endowed Baymouth with a size it did not possess. For all its quaint sandstone buildings lining its modest main street, it had never laid claim to such an honor. Even in the days when its Norman church had been young, the stained glass in the north transept new, and the Latin inscription over the door still legible, it had been little more than a hamlet. But it was a picturesque and charming village for all that.

Caroline looked around with approval as she alighted from the carriage.

Annie, descending from the vehicle after Melissa, was no connoisseur of scenic places. Her first question was a blunt "Do you think they have an inn about that boasts a good table? Or even," she lowered her standards reluctantly, "a quite mediocre one would serve. I am almost famished."

"We shall deal with the matter of food later. Just now we must go to the linen drapers and purchase some suitable material for Melissa's gowns. After that we will see the dressmaker and possibly the milliner."

Annie, disconsolate at the knowledge that food would not be forthcoming, managed a grim nod. She plodded along after Caroline and Melissa, giving brief, wistful glances backward when they passed an establishment that sold or served any type of food.

"I wish it were not necessary to wear black," Melissa said as they stopped outside the linen drapers. Her eyes wandered to a tangerine taffeta cloth displayed in the window beside a blue kerseymere.

"I know this is a very difficult time in your life, Melissa," Caroline said gently, "but you must remember that once your mourning is over you can be properly introduced to London society. Of course you can't have a come-out, but you will be able to enjoy wearing any number of fine clothes. Your husband has left you in a very enviable position, you know."

"A widow?" Melissa asked innocently, turning her wide green eyes on Caroline in an expression of surprise.

"I mean he has left you with a good deal of money after his untimely death," Caroline clarified.

"Oh."

"But for now, of course, you must dress as befits a widow."

Melissa murmured her agreement as they stepped into the shop. But once inside her resolution was forgotten among the bolts and bolts of material and her eyes roved from a bright rose length of satin to a jewel-green muslin."

"Black, dear," Caroline reminded her. Her niece nodded obediently, although her eyes clung to a ravishing turquoise silk for a moment.

"There will be time enough later for such gowns," Caroline consoled gently.

Privately she thought it was indeed lamentable that a sixteen-year-old girl should be forced to go into a year's mourning. True, her husband was dead, but in this case the mourning period exceeded the length of the marriage. And Caroline felt certain Melissa had never loved the late earl, although she had probably liked him well enough. After all, what did a young girl know of love?

Why, she herself had never yet met the man she could fall in love with. And she had met a great many eligible men in London during her come-out. That blissful state was something of a myth, she considered, as she touched a piece of saffron poplin.

"I should like this one," Melissa called from behind a stack of bolts; and Caroline put the thought of love and men from her mind to deal with the far more pressing concern of fashion.

CHAPTER 7

Caroline fingered the lace of her white shawl as she walked along, stepping carefully over the jagged fragments of rocks that now and again interrupted her progress. To her left she could look down and see the ocean beating an entreaty against the base of the cliffs; to her right the rolling hills of the hinterland with their gentle, sheltering combes drew a peaceful and serene pastoral picture.

The skies were clear and balmy, blowing through her short copper hair with a crisp breeze from the ocean. Now and again she stopped to gaze out across its vast blueness before turning to continue, swinging her bonnet from its ribbons as she walked.

In truth, Caroline could not fully appreciate the beauty of the scenery about her. Her mind was far too preoccupied considering the events of the morning's interview with Mr. Mortimer, the solicitor handling Chester's estate.

He had made it perfectly obvious he disapproved of the late earl's will. But when Caroline had asked whether he had been visited by Lord Devlon, the solicitor had raised bushy gray eyebrows and said "Most certainly not," in a strangled voice of outrage.

"I would not," he had informed her majestically, "discuss the contents of a will with someone who was not mentioned in that document."

"Even if he was a brother and one who would hope to inherit the family estate?" Caroline pressed. Beside her she sensed Melissa shifting uncomfortably in her chair and looking toward the door with longing.

Mr. Mortimer had straightened his slight shoulders, hunched farther forward on his cluttered desk, and peered at Caroline through the gloom of his dark, furniture-crowded office. "Young lady, I hope I know how to conduct my business."

He hunched even farther forward—the man was a habitual huncher, Caroline reflected—but she had been gratified by his answer. At least he had not been won over by Lord Devlon. The old solicitor's next words had shaken her newfound complacency.

"I've known Rye since he was a boy in leading strings," he declared, hunching dangerously. "I can vouch that he will do nothing to embarrass the family name. Furthermore it is good he has come to Hollowsby to help your niece in these trying times. You should be exceedingly grateful; he will protect you from the sharp tongues of gossip." His final glowering look had fallen on Melissa as if to say he thought she was in need of such protection.

"Rye has a fortune in his own right—mother's money, I collect. And he's a shrewd businessman as well. He doesn't care about this estate because of the money, I'll be bound. He is only assuring himself that no dishonor comes to his family home. Don't you agree?" he had demanded peremptorily.

"I quite agree he is shrewd," Caroline had replied as she rose to leave.

She pulled her shawl tighter around her as a fresh gust of wind whipped in from the ocean. As she traipsed through the tall grass toward a grove of trees, Caroline looked around at the beauty of the countryside once again.

She stopped abruptly as she spied something black bounding through the long green grass. Shading her eyes with a hand, she stared intently. What sort of animal jumped up and down like that when it ran? It was far too large to be a squirrel or a rabbit. As it neared, she saw it was even larger than she had thought. It appeared to be the size of—

"Oh, dear Lord," Caroline breathed as she realized with belated certainty that it was Clover.

Turning again toward the grove of trees, she dropped her bonnet and picked up her cream poplin skirts. Then she showed the dog a pair of heels she would not have thought herself capable of. Running with all her might toward the trees, she turned her head back only now and again to check the progress of her pursuer. Clover, she noted with rising alarm, was gaining on her with uncomfortable speed. She turned back toward her goal, setting her mind to the race with a new fervor.

As she neared the little clump of trees, she counted them rapidly. It was a difficult task, since they moved back and forth and up and down in time with the jogging of her movements but she thought there were five. As she sped toward the trees she looked for one with a low enough branch to swing herself up into.

Panting heavily, she threw a hurried glance over her shoulder. The sight that met her eyes wrenched a gasp of fear from her already nearly breathless lungs. There, not five feet behind her, teeth bared to reveal an outline of white, sharpened points and ears laid back in a primitive expression of the hunter, was Clover.

Caroline darted into the grove of trees, reaching upward and catching a low branch as she ran. She let her feet fly off the ground and swung herself upward. In just a moment, she thought frantically, she would be safely up in the tree. She felt a sickening lurch as her progress was halted in mid-air. Clover had her.

Caroline sat on a limb high up in the small tree and ruefully surveyed the back of her torn skirt. She looked down at the dog contently stretched beneath the tree and gave herself over to wrathful thoughts about him. Why didn't Melissa keep the cur on a leash? Better yet, why didn't she set him adrift on a boat on the ocean? But then again, she considered waspishly, drowning was far too good for him.

Caroline's dignity was only slightly less damaged than her gown, the back of which was in shreds. And if she was forced to remain perched on this uncomfortable limb much longer, it did not bode well for her feelings toward either Clover or Melissa.

Looking down again, she made a face at Clover from her safe position seven feet above him. But even with that buffer area, the sight of the large black creature was still unnerving. She gave a shiver of discomfort as she recalled the fear she had felt when she heard his gnashing teeth take firm hold of her skirts. It had been necessary to sacrifice the gown, pretty cream poplin though it was, as well as a considerable part of her new lawn petticoat, to hoist herself out of his clutches.

And what was worse, Caroline thought fretfully, she had been in the tree for well above an hour and Clover showed not the least sign of leaving. What if he didn't leave at all? she wondered with a tremor of panic. She might even be forced to stay here all night. Surely, she reasoned, he would become hungry eventually and return to the house. In the meantime she could do nothing but wait.

Clover and Melissa, she considered as she settled back on the limb, were the best of friends so Clover must like *some* humans. It was only because he had thought she was trespassing that he did not like her. But she wasn't, of course; she was merely walking on Hollowsby land. Therefore, it seemed reasonable that she had only to make friends with the animal and surely he would let her pass. Then she could return to the house and make plans for his removal to a suitably drafty cellar in a ratless basement, she thought vengefully.

As if Clover could read her thoughts, he looked up and gave a lazy growl of dominance before returning to his sleeping position.

"Nice doggy," Caroline called down. She thought the beseeching note in her voice masked her contempt for him quite effectively. Apparently Clover didn't; he made no reply.

Venturing down a limb lower, Caroline carefully seated herself again. "I don't dislike animals, you know," she confided. "I was only out for a walk and . . ." This was ridiculous. The stupid dog was not paying the least heed to her, and she felt excessively foolish.

She was taking altogether the wrong approach with the cur, she fumed. She would simply be masterful and he would let her pass. Still, she had to admit, it was hard to appear as if she had the situation well in hand while clinging to an upper branch. Clover seemed aware of that as he flicked a bored glance in her direction before returning once again to his nap.

Caroline looked around in distraction. What was she going to do? She suspected few people ever passed this way. Melissa was the only one likely to come looking for Clover, and that might not be for some time. Raising her face to scan the horizon, she affirmed with dismal certainty that she was indeed alone.

But wait. . . . What was that dot on the horizon? Wasn't it moving?

Peering toward the faint black speck, she discerned it *was* moving. In fact as she watched, it grew steadily larger. When it came into full view, she could see that it was a horse with a rider. Her hopes soared and she leaned forward in the tree. Help was on the way. But who was it?

For answer the rider moved toward the trees and

his form became even more pronounced. The unparalleled beauty of a magnificent chestnut horse carrying a rider with a proud set to his shoulder combined to give her a picture of one man. It was the earl.

"It wanted only this," she muttered, "to make my day complete. First I am nearly eaten by a dog, and now I am to be roasted and made sport of by the earl of Devlon, no less."

For one impetuous moment Caroline considered remaining motionless in the tree and making no attempt to gain the earl's attention. But that, she concluded miserably, would serve no purpose. She would only spite herself. No, she must attract his notice.

She raised her voice in a cry for help, but the wind, blowing strongly toward her, carried it back to her. There was scant chance he would hear her, she realized. Well, these were desperate times and desperate actions were called for, she concluded. Slowly, regretfully, she pulled her maligned petticoat off and crawled as far out on the limb as she dared. Then, holding it in the air and letting the wind catch it, she waved the white flag of surrender and entreaty.

"Are you satisfied?" she called down to the sleeping dog as she frantically waved her banner. "The earl shall laugh for weeks over this."

Unmoved, Clover continued to nap.

Caroline watched the rider intently as he drew his horse up and looked in her direction; but he was not close enough for her to see the expression on his face. Surely he would not think it was a mast blown up from some fishing boat and ride on past. She prayed that he wouldn't and breathed a sigh of relief as she saw him turn his horse toward the grove. He approached with maddening slowness. Finally he was close enough to be within hearing distance.

Still waving her petticoat, she cried. "My lord! Help me!"

Lord Devlon reached the trees and swung off his horse. After tying the chestnut to a tree, he said a few short words to Clover that sent the fearsome dog cowering into the tall grass.

"You may come down now, Miss Norton," he directed in emotionless accents.

She descended slowly. "Clover chased me to this tree and—"

"I believe I can deduce what happened."

Caroline looked at him closely. Was it her imagination or was there the faintest twitching of muscles at the corner of his mouth? He was laughing at her!

"I suppose you think it ever so amusing," she accused him sullenly as she thrust her petticoat behind her with one hand and straightened her rumpled skirts with her other.

His lips parted into a slow grin. "I must own I never thought to be summoned by you in quite this manner. I was, however, once invited to a rather bawdy household by a female waving a pair of silk stockings from an upper window," he recalled with a wicked gleam in his eye.

"I should have known you would make sport of the whole incident," she snapped. "How would you have liked to have been forced to swing from a limb for endless hours while a wild creature held you at bay?"

"The dog appeared to be asleep when I arrived," he noted mildly.

"Well, he was not asleep an hour back," she retorted. "He chased me with great speed and—" she broke off. "I consider it very unhandsome of you to laugh."

"You are right, of course. It is wrong of me. You are a lady in distress, and I should act the part of a knight on a white horse. Are you hurt?"

She resolutely blinked back the tears of humiliation that crowded unbidden into her eyes. "No, but my gown is ruined."

"Don't cry. It wasn't your best gown, was it?" he asked in an attempt to win her away from tears.

"It is all very well for you to laugh but it was not *your* gown that was eaten," she replied, unmollified by his bantering, friendly tone.

Lord Devlon manfully suppressed a smile and answered gravely. "Indeed, it was not. But then, Clover can scarcely be blamed for taking his meals where he can find them. I daresay the cloth of your gown was as appetizing as anything he has had in some time if he eats the same food we do."

He moved closer to her, taking her hand in his. "You're shaking, Miss Norton." A look of concern crossed his face as he peered closer at her. "Are you certain you have suffered no ill effects?"

She lowered her lashes and regarded his starched cravat. Something about the intense blueness of his eyes prevented her from looking directly into them.

"Only my dress and my pride are wounded," she said in a small voice.

"I am sorry, Miss Norton." This time genuine contrition rang in his voice. "I should not have laughed at your situation. The dog could have done you a serious injury. Here." Taking off his caped riding coat, he wrapped it about her. "You will be more comfortable in my presence if you have my coat over your torn gown."

"Thank you," she murmured.

"Did the dog bite you? Show me where."

Her relief at being rescued and her embarrassment combined to create a most unladylike sense of the ridiculous. Had Clover bitten her she could scarcely have shown him where! She shook her head. "He did not," she said, a small smile betraying her thoughts.

The earl stood staring down at Caroline without speaking. For the briefest of moments, when the smile had played across her delicate face, he had experienced a sensation he had never felt before. It was one that might have been akin to, although not the same as, fascination. He had never thought to see such an enchanting smile from the stiff Miss Norton.

She checked and regarded him curiously. "Did I say something wrong, my lord? You had the oddest look on your face."

He recovered himself swiftly. "No, of course not."

"Well, that's all right then. I shouldn't like to offend you, my lord, as I am ever so grateful you found me. I had despaired of being rescued at all," she confided.

He nodded. "Come, I will put you on my horse."

Lord Devlon lifted her into the saddle and mounted behind her, then turned the chestnut toward the house. As it carried them with easy strides, Caroline was conscious of the hard beating of the earl's heart against her cheek. She flushed at the thought.

"Are you cold, Miss Norton?"

"No, thank you, I am fine."

"Have you been gone from the house long? Someone may be worried about you."

"There is only Melissa, and I shouldn't think she will have noticed that I am gone."

He nodded and lapsed into silence.

Caroline was so close to the earl that when he breathed it stirred little curls around her ear. It was a situation she found flustering yet strangely satisfying. At any rate, she did not turn her head to avoid it. It was odd, she considered, that she was nestled so comfortably against Lord Devlon when only the other night she had thought what a cold man he was. Now he did not seem so. There was a gentleness in the way he held her, as if he were almost afraid he would crush her. She liked being held that way. In a vain effort to rouse herself to feel uncomfortable in his arms, she reminded herself of the unpleasant things he had said to her when they arrived. At the present, however, the memory of those words seemed hazy. All she was certain of was that Lord Devlon was holding her in his arms and she did not object.

CHAPTER 8

Caroline stood beside the door of the purple bedroom as she concluded her irate tale of the ill use to which she had been subjected by the creature now lying blissfully on the bed.

"Clover meant no harm," Melissa assured her aunt as she lay beside her pet and stroked his black fur. Clover, lying on the bed beneath the purple canopy, looked quite pleased with himself. He accepted Melissa's affectionate pats with polite forbearance, like royalty recognizing the adulation of the masses as something of a bore but entirely their due.

Caroline gave the dog a withering look and said sternly, "I daresay, he did not; but harm has been done nonetheless." She permitted herself another rueful glance at her tattered gown and petticoat. Recalling the use to which the petticoat had been put in an effort to summon help, Caroline blushed furiously and steeled herself to speak again, overcoming her momentary lapse of will in the face of Melissa's cajoling words. "Clover has shown himself an untrustworthy animal. He would do an injury to anyone who ventured across the pasture. I think he should not be allowed to roam free," she ended.

Melissa's eyes widened at her aunt's words. "Whatever do you mean?"

"He should be kept on a leash."

"But if he is not permitted outside of the house, he could do no harm," Melissa protested. "Why couldn't I just keep him in the house all the time?"

"The house is the very place he should no longer be permitted *inside* of," Caroline pronounced. "And," she added, "I also believe he should be removed from this bedroom, so that it can be prepared for human occupation."

"But that isn't necessary. Everyone has a room already."

"Guests might arrive at any time," Caroline pointed out reasonably. "And, as to that, the dark little room I have been given does not compare with this room. Why, mine doesn't even have a sitting room adjoining it."

"Clover has always occupied this room."

Sinking down into a gilt-framed chair, Caroline continued in rational tones. "My dear, I think it behooves us to behave with as much respectability as possible. Don't you agree?"

Melissa softly stroked Clover's ears and mumbled "Yes" while the dog gave a sigh of contentment and rolled onto his back.

Caroline repressed her exasperation and continued: "I advise you to give serious consideration to housing Clover somewhere else—someplace that is more in keeping with where a dog should be kept."

"But Auntie Caro, he wouldn't be happy anywhere else. His feelings are quite delicate and he would be very hurt if he was moved elsewhere. If you could know him as I do, you would like him ever so much better," Melissa noted hopefully.

"I do not wish to know him any better. As it is, he and I know each other quite well enough. After all, he is the only dog ever to see my petticoats, let alone chew at them. I think that is quite a close enough acquaintance," Caroline finished with a glare at the dog lying happily atop the counterpane of the bed.

"You aren't angry with Clover, are you?" Melissa pressed. "He meant no harm."

"I am not best pleased with him, but that is over now and can't be helped. I am going to my room to change, but I think you should give thought to my advice concerning Clover. I hope you come to some suitable arrangement."

With those words Caroline turned and walked back toward her own bedroom. She paused only long enough in the hall to knock on Annie's door, silently berating the lack of a working bell system in the house. Then she continued on to her room to await Annie's arrival.

Her maid appeared at her door moments later. "Did you want me, ma'am?"

"Yes, I wish to prepare for bed."

At Annie's doubtful look Caroline continued, "It is early, but I find I had a rather tiresome day and I am fatigued." Turning, she presented her back to the maid. "Help me out of this gown, please."

Annie approached slowly, wonder in her voice. "Did you know that your gown is torn in the back?"

"Yes, I did," Caroline gritted out in a voice held to a moderate volume only by a superb effort of will.

Annie fingered the material. "It looks like the work of a witch. They sometimes cast spells on people and play such tricks. Even the petticoat is frayed," she announced as she investigated further. "It is surely the work of a witch."

"It is the work of Clover," Caroline explained tartly. "He saw me crossing the meadow and gave chase. I only reached a tree in time."

"Then it may not be as bad as I thought," Annie encouraged. "A strange dog following a person is a sign of good luck."

Caroline greeted that bit of folk wisdom with an annihilating look. "Don't be a goose. There is nothing strange about Clover except that he wants to eat people. And I scarcely see how you can call hanging from the limb of a tree for an hour any sort of luck."

"Well, then it is the work of a witch, as I said. The witch," she announced with a significant look at Caroline, "has taken the shape of a dog." Her eyes lighted in her small, wrinkled face as she continued. "Have you ever noticed what black eyes he has and how mean looking they are? Just like the eyes of a witch. Or a warlock." She made generous allowance for Clover's sex.

"I'm sure I have never noted Clover's eyes, Annie, but I have not paid so very much attention to him as I might have. Although," Caroline added dryly, "I had ample time to study him today."

"I am almost sure of it. Witches have a certain look about the eyes, you know, and Clover has that very look. He should be got rid of."

"I couldn't agree more," Caroline replied with a yawn. But just now she had more important considerations on her mind, specifically, the problem of finding a companion for Melissa.

Caroline stepped out of her ruined dress and allowed Annie to help her into a thin white chemise that draped softly on her slender frame. Her thoughts were still directed toward her niece. Melissa, she argued with herself, was only a bit misguided. She could be molded into a perfectly proper young lady if someone merely took the time and trouble to do so. But Caroline knew of no acceptable matron to undertake such a task.

Her mind drifted further afield, to thoughts of the earl as she had nestled in his arms on the ride back to Hollowsby. Of course, his actions had been born of necessity. Still, she derived a peculiar satisfaction from the memory of the moment when he had swept her off her feet and into the saddle.

Annie laid back the covers of the bed, happily disclosing a cure for overcoming the evil eye as she worked, but Caroline heard few of her maid's words. Her eyes wandered absently to the open doors of the wardrobe. Her clothes, she considered, were a bit out of fashion. She had not been to London shopping in some time and the dresses she had had made in Wiltshire were not entirely à la mode. Perhaps she should send to London for some fashion plates and fabrics for new gowns.

Caroline caught herself in surprise, straightening abruptly. Whatever was putting such thoughts into her head?

"Yes, I knew that would shock you," Annie said, noting her mistress's response with satisfaction, "but it's true, for all that. A live toad held in the mouth can cure chin-cough."

Caroline was oblivious to the medicinal wonders of the toad. She was following her own train of thought. Send to London indeed! Who was she rigging herself out to attract?

Still when she lay down to sleep a short time later, happy visions of new gowns and pelisses paraded before her in stylish abundance, and she wore them with a grace that turned men's heads. It was a particularly agreeable dream and one which she would have been content to explore further. Such was not to be the case, however, for she was awakened when the sound of a great crash brought her bolt upright in the darkened room. She listened intently, but when the noise was not repeated, she threw back the bed covers and sprang up. Tossing her ruffled white peignoir over her chemise, she picked up her taper and tinderbox and hurried out into the hall.

There she spied two small flames of light bobbing toward her as she hastily lighted her own candle.

"Auntie Caro, are you all right?" Melissa's shaken voice demanded. "I heard a dreadful noise!"

"I'm fine. I heard the sound also; I believe it came from your end of the hall."

"Miss Norton is right," the earl's unmistakable

voice agreed. "It was from somewhere in the vicinity of my grandfather's bust."

He broke off with a muttered curse just as Caroline reached the spot where he and Melissa stood. Looking downward in the gloomy light of the candles, she beheld the source of his anger. There, splintered into a thousand pieces upon the floor, lay the remnants of what must have been a very fine bust.

"How could it have fallen?" Melissa asked in wonder.

"It didn't fall," the earl grated out. He thrust his candle into Caroline's hand. "Hold it steady," he commanded as he bent to examine the marble column the bust had stood upon. "There's nothing amiss with it," he noted, rising and taking his candle back. "It is perfectly obvious it was dropped."

"Surely it was knocked off by someone passing in the hall. Perhaps they were groping their way along in the dark," Caroline suggested. "Why would someone be carrying such a large bust? It looks like it is quite heavy."

"It *was* quite heavy." The look Lord Devlon directed at Caroline was fraught with impatience discernible even in the uncertain light of the candles. "I fancy it would have taken a Cyclops walking past such a large bust to knock it off. Besides," he added dampeningly, "unless it was the Cyclops Ulysses blinded, I fail to see why he would have been groping his way down the hall rather than using a candle like everyone else."

"Cyclopes are very unpredictable," Caroline retorted.

He turned back toward the shattered statue and continued, "It was dropped by someone in the process of stealing it."

"Merciful heavens!" Annie exclaimed, arriving on the scene like a small whirlwind. "This is by everything awful! The person that bust was made from will die within a sennight; nothing can be done to stop the curse. It's worse than dropping a picture of a person," she moaned, wringing her hands.

"The man is already dead," Lord Devlon informed her brusquely.

"I knew it!" Annie shouted morosely. "But there was nothing that could have saved him once the bust was dropped. Although," she added, "I did not expect him to die so soon afterward. They usually live a few days."

"He has been dead these fifty years past," Lord Devlon snapped.

"Don't you speak that way to my maid," Caroline entered the lists. "She doesn't have to toadeat you."

"I wonder if that's where the cure came from?" Annie asked, much struck by the thought. "Of course for chin-cough, you don't actually *eat* the toad. You just hold it in your mouth. Still, it's very similar, don't you think?"

Lord Devlon muttered an inaudible but pithy expletive and turned. "I will look around the house to determine if anyone is about. I suggest all of you return to your rooms."

Caroline did as she was bid but her remaining hours of sleep were destined to be restless.

When she greeted the earl the following morning

at the breakfast table, she was in a decidedly unpleasant mood. It was shortly to become a good deal worse.

Lord Devlon's first words were inauspicious. "I have looked about the house and have discovered there are some family heirlooms missing—small vases, statues, jeweled swords, and the like. Some of them have been in my family for generations. They are of great antiquity and would fetch quite a nice price at Sotheby's."

Caroline looked up in surprise, her knife suspended in the act of applying marmalade to her toast.

"I have spoken with the servants and they have no knowledge of the location of these heirlooms. However, they did say the articles were never ordered removed for safekeeping. Frederick assures me they were present until the day I arrived," he concluded with a challenging stare at Caroline.

She met his look blankly. "Are you implying that I might have taken something from this house?"

"I am implying nothing. I am asking."

"How dare you!" Caroline bristled. "I take leave to tell you I find you the most odious, ill-mannered, mean-spirited man it has ever been my misfortune to meet!"

"That's all very interesting," he snapped, "but hardly to the point. I wish to hear from your own lips what you know about these treasures."

"I know nothing! If they are gone, then, I assure you someone greedier than I has taken them."

"There is no one greedier than you," he told her

calmly. "Can you explain why they disappeared the same day you arrived?"

No," she replied coldly.

"Would you allow me to search your room?"

"Certainly not!" Caroline met his hard, accusing gaze levelly.

"Then I can only assume you have something to hide, Miss Norton."

"I confess!" Goaded, she wadded her napkin up and threw it onto the table. "I stole them and secreted them in the folds of my linen. I was planning to ship them to Italy or some other fascinating place my governess spoke of when I was learning my globes. I was going to buy a villa and live reclusively. I was on my way to a comfortable life," she concluded with a defiant toss of her head that sent her copper curls dancing.

"You are on your way to Newgate prison," he expostulated.

While Caroline regarded the earl's stony countenance with a cold fury of her own, something righted itself in her head. "What if I had taken anything?" she asked archly. "It is no concern of yours. My niece has inherited this house and all its contents."

"You may think so if it pleases you," he told her in quelling tones, "but you will shortly learn differently. I have had enough of trying to use reason with you. It is clear you are not a reasonable woman. I shall now use whatever measures are necessary to regain my property."

"You must do as you think fit, I'm sure, my lord," she replied with hauteur.

"If I did so, I should be tried for murder," he muttered.

Caroline gave him a scathing look, then returned to her food. Actually she was far from hungry, but she refused to retreat from the battlefield.

Beside her, Lord Devlon was certainly in no better humor. He picked up the hand bell and rang it so furiously that Caroline was forced to put a hand over her ear.

"What do I have to do to get a glass of water?" he demanded irritably when no servant appeared.

"Why don't you try setting yourself afire, my lord," Caroline suggested with an acidic smile.

He rose abruptly. "I am going to London, Miss Norton, and when I come back, I shall have all the evidence to shatter your niece's claim to this house or any part of my brother's estate. Enjoy yourself while you may. I shall speak with you upon my return."

"I live in anticipation of that moment," came the haughty response.

CHAPTER 9

Lord Devlon reined in his horse and gazed down the long lane. The trip to London had been a tiresome journey and the roads had been worse than he had expected. He didn't wish to prolong his trip any longer than necessary. Still, he considered, it was possible the man who lived in the house at the end of this road could offer further information.

What the earl had learned thus far had been most unsettling. Miss Norton, he had discovered upon making a few discreet inquiries, was a companion. At that thought his mouth tightened in anger. No wonder she was so anxious to come to Hollowsby. Doubtless she had been a poorly-paid servant to some aging dowager. She had been very careful to make no mention to him of her former position. Rather, she seemed to have been at great pains to hide it.

And if that was not bad enough, Miss Norton's sister had lived with half of the men in Europe. Why, they were a veritable tribe of adventuresses! It was easy to see why the child had made such an unsuitable marriage: she had had precious little example.

The earl gazed down the muddy lane again. With a resigned movement he turned his horse toward the house. Damn. He might as well learn all there was to know. Roxby and Chester had been the closest of friends, so it was possible Roxby had met Melissa and knew something about her. At the thought of the pretty but mindless young widow, Lord Devlon silently berated his brother. How could Chester have married such a child? Had he no sense of his position? It was one thing to have a woman in keeping—one old enough to know her own mind at that—but it was entirely reprehensible to marry a chit that young.

He splatted down the muddy lane to the Baroque-style house set at the end. There he reined in his horse, slid from the saddle, and walked up the tall flight of steps to the first floor. Taking hold of the knocker, he gave it a hard bang.

The door swung open and a shriveled butler surveyed the mud-covered visitor critically, as if debating whether to admit him into the house.

"Giles, is that you?" Lord Devlon greeted the old man with amiable surprise. "I thought you had stuck your spoon into the wall ages since."

"The good rarely die young, Master Bythestone," the stooped old man told him ominously, inspecting his lordship with a keen look that seemed to say he expected the earl to expire at any moment.

"I suspect you have the right of it," he agreed affably. "I haven't been in such top fettle of late."

"Exactly so." Giles nodded in satisfaction.

"Is Roxby home?"

"Indeed, my lord. He is in the parlor."

"I'll announce myself," the earl said, taking off his coat and handing it to Giles, who received it after bestowing a woeful look at his immaculate white gloves. "I fancy I still remember where the parlor is. Is Roxby alone?"

"He is. There was," Giles coughed his disapproval, "a certain female with him, but she left this morning."

"Shocking!" Lord Devlon said, a sentiment belied by his grin as he turned toward the parlor. Stalking to it, he flung the door open and stepped into a small room heavy with smoke and crowded with overstuffed chairs. Across the room Lord Devlon saw the back of a graying head. It had a patch of baldness, which had grown larger since the earl had seen it last.

"Damn you, man. I've told you to knock before you enter. And if it's company you're announcing, tell them I'm not at home."

"Tell me yourself, Roxby," Lord Devlon laughed.

The portly man turned in his chair and then brought a monocle up to one eye. "That you, Rye?"

"It is."

"Impertinent as ever, ain't you?"

"I am."

"Well, don't just stand there with the door open, come in for God's sake. You're creating a hell of a draft."

I could not fail to honor such a gracious invitation," Lord Devlon said as he closed the door and entered the room. "How have you been?"

"Bloody awful."

"I am sorry to hear that."

"Poppycock! You couldn't care less about my health. I'll warrant you didn't drive off the Exeter road on your way to London to pursue your wenching just to ask after my health. Well, out with it! What is it you want?"

"I am returning from London, not going," Lord Devlon corrected mildly as he crossed to the mantel and leaned casually against it.

"How are the women?" Roxby asked with a glimmer of interest in his eyes. "I haven't been to London these three years past. I have wondered now and again if the women are as prime as ever."

"More so," Lord Devlon assured him.

"Ahh, I thought they would be." The older man relaxed back in his chair and sighed. "I must get up to London."

"You are as lecherous as ever, I see."

"A man must have his pleasures. Well, sit down, don't just stand there like some sort of village halfwit."

"Thank you, but I could hardly have seated myself without being invited to do so," Lord Devlon remarked as he sank into a green velvet chair.

"You stopped by my house uninvited," Roxby reminded him bluntly.

"But I have some business I wish to discuss with you."

"What is it? You don't want money, do you? I won't let you have any, you know, so you might just as well take yourself off."

Undeterred by his host's lack of hospitality, the

earl pursued. "My brother was married to a very young girl. Did you ever meet her or know the circumstances of that marriage?"

"Terrible thing about Chester. Terrible. Hated to see him go. I meant to attend the funeral but my gout, you know. Terrible," Roxby lamented, picking up a glass from the table by his side as he spoke. "Port," he explained simply. "Care for any?"

"No, thank you. I shan't be staying long. I merely wished to discuss the matter of Chester's marriage."

"Pretty little piece, though a bit empty in the upper works." Roxby pointed a finger at his head. "Still, one can't expect everything in a wife."

"You knew her?"

"Only briefly. Chester brought her here when they were on their way to Hollowsby after the wedding."

"That is what I particularly wished to speak with you about. I had thought the wedding took place at St. George's in London. But I could find no church record of it."

Roxby shifted in his chair, regarding his glass intently. "Could you not? Oh well, such things are often destroyed, eaten by church mice—they're notoriously voracious eaters, you know. Any number of things could have happened to it." He dismissed the subject with a shrug.

Lord Devlon eyed his host speculatively. "That appears passing strange, since records for other marriages performed that day were present. Don't you think it unusual that all the other records would be there and my brother's missing?"

"Hard to explain some things." Roxby dismissed

the mystery and turned to a careful examination of his fingernails.

"Yes, it is." The earl rose. "I believe I will just have a glass of that port you mentioned."

His host jerked his head toward a decanter on a gateleg table by the fireplace. "Help yourself."

Lord Devlon poured a glass, returned with the decanter and refilled Roxby's glass before seating himself across from the older man.

"How have your cattle been running?" he asked conversationally.

Roxby gave him a suspicious look, which was met with a bland smile. "Bought a prime bit of blood only last week," he began slowly. Before long he fell into a pleasant monologue, describing the next run at Newmarket, the new cut of men's fashions and the rising young pugilist who had trained with both Cribb and Jackson. As he talked the port flowed liberally, with Lord Devlon keeping it on the table by his side and frequently filling his host's glass. Gradually the subject turned to women and then to the late earl's marriage.

"Gel was a pretty piece," Roxby observed, blinking into the fireplace and trying unsuccessfully to stifle a hiccup.

"She was."

"Liked her a lot, even if her mother was the biggest trollop in the country."

"Likable girl," Lord Devlon agreed cordially.

"Bit of an empty-headed chit, but I don't think Chester married her for intellectual companionship." Roxby gave a bawdy laugh.

"He didn't."

"Liquor don't loosen your tongue much, does it, Rye?" the older man observed with a disgruntled look at his companion.

"Not apparently as much as it does yours," Lord Devlon replied with a smile.

"It don't loosen mine to the point that I divulge secrets," his host said with a sly look toward Lord Devlon to see if he would take the bait. When the earl merely continued to sip his port, Roxby added, "I could tell you any number of tales. But I won't, because I ain't the type to talk just because I've had a glassful or two of spirits."

"You've had five."

"You counting?" Roxby asked with a sharp look at his guest.

"No, of course not."

"Could tell you some interesting stories," the older man continued, his words slurring slightly, "but I'm a man of honor, gave my word and all."

"There is only one tale I wish to hear," Lord Devlon said pleasantly, swirling his drink in his glass and watching it with interest. "And that is about the bogus marriage that took place right here in this parlor less than a year ago."

Roxby set his glass down hastily, overcome by a sudden fit of choking.

Lord Devlon waited politely for it to subside before pursuing, "You've never suffered from the smallest touch of gout, Roxby. But you couldn't go to Chester's funeral, either, could you? Even the grieving widow would have recognized the bishop who married her."

"Who told you? I'll kill that self-righteous Giles!" Roxby made an attempt to rise to accomplish that mission, but the strain was too much and he slumped back into his chair. "I'll do it later," he said with a limp gesture of his hand.

"Giles did not tell me. But it is obvious the marriage did not take place in the church Chester so kindly wrote me of. Odd, that. I hadn't heard from my brother in half a dozen years. And then he wrote me a chatty note describing his wedding ceremony. Don't you find that singular?"

"Lovely wedding. Stands to reason he wanted to tell you all about it." Roxby suddenly found the rug a source of intense interest.

Lord Devlon continued, "I take leave to doubt he found himself possessed of a fierce desire to share the details of his wedding with me. I rather think he merely thought to flummery me into believing there *had been* a wedding. You were his best friend, so it stands to reason he might have asked you to be a witness. But then, he needed a bishop more than he needed a witness, didn't he?"

Roxby shifted in the chair and mumbled. "It can do no harm to tell you now. No, there never was a marriage. But Chester wanted to marry the chit and her mother was not to be found to give permission. In the end, he decided to just make the child think they were married. And he was very good to her," he noted defensively. "He included her in his will, so no harm was done in the long run."

Lord Devlon rose and set his drink down with a harsh clatter. "On the contrary, a great harm has been done. As his *widow* the girl would have inherited Hollowsby and a deal of money. As his *mistress,* she is not mentioned in the will. And Hollowsby is one thing I will not stand by and see taken from me."

"But you can't turn the child out in the cold!" Roxby protested, his face turning red and his hands turning white as they grasped the arms of the chair tightly. "Chester would have married her if the mother could have been found. As it was, he put the word about that they were married so no one would ever question it. Let the girl keep her title and you can buy the house from her. Good Lord, Rye, what can paying her for the old ruins signify?"

"She won't sell the old ruins,'" Lord Devlon said bitterly.

"Make her sell! She's only a girl. Surely you can manage her. You always had a way with women."

The earl stalked to the door. "She is no doubt manageable, but her reinforcements are not so easily controlled. There is an aunt in residence who doubtless means to make the most of this to gain whatever she can from it for herself and her niece. Good day, Roxby."

He collected his hat on the way out, leaving Giles to deal with the apoplexy Roxby showed signs of having. Outside, he mounted his horse and rode off down the road, while the jumble of thoughts in his brain began to sort themselves out. His anger at his brother was pointless, he knew. Chester was dead and nothing could change that. But his feelings toward Melissa were altered; she had clearly been duped. And what of her aunt? Had he misjudged her too?

Damn the fates! It would have been entirely different if Miss Courtney had been a party to this outrageous scheme. Then he could order her from the house—quite obviously his house now—with a clear conscience. And her aunt as well.

But it was much more complicated than that. His brother had behaved in an abominable manner. And Chester's pathetic attempt to make up for his hoax by willing Hollowsby to Melissa had only embroiled her deeper in a muddle.

If Chester had left her only his money, Lord Devlon would have been content to let it pass. In fact, he would have considered it his duty as a gentleman not to say anything to embarrass the child and bring to light his brother's indiscretion. But Hollowsby was beyond everything too much!

As the horse's hooves pounding on the road brought him ever closer to the estate, his mind continued to whirl. Regardless of Melissa's right to the property, there was the matter of the priceless objects that were missing. The fact still held that they had begun to disappear the day of Miss Norton's arrival. It was an occurrence that made her look very suspicious. Perhaps, after all, he ought not concern himself with the question of how to remove the pair from the house delicately. Maybe he should simply present them with the knowledge he now held, explain that Melissa had not inherited the veriest farthing, and order them both from Hollowsby.

That would be the most expedient solution to the problem, and it could hardly be considered ungentlemanly to take whatever measures were necessary to prevent his family home from falling into the hands of those who could well be termed gypsies. Even Miss Norton, for all her refinements, *had* been a companion. And she had lost no time resigning her position when she thought she saw a more comfortable life opening up to her.

The horse continued to beat out a tattoo on the road and the gates of Hollowsby loomed ever nearer. As Lord Devlon approached, he was still undecided as to the best course of action. And when he tried to sort the matter out logically, he was hampered by irrelevant thoughts of how beguiling Caroline had looked with her copper hair tossed by the wind, her cheeks crimson with embarrassment, and her dress ruined by a dog.

CHAPTER 10

Caroline unobtrusively studied the man on the curricle seat beside her as he expertly handled the reins, controlling his spirited bays with ease. Lord Devlon looked much the same as he had when he had left for London five days ago. He was dressed in a Bath green coat and buff-colored pantaloons. His crisp, white cravat was a study of good grooming and his Hessians held the subtle gloss of many buffings. In short, his appearance was as impeccable as it had always been. But some difference had been wrought in him that Caroline could not account for. His attitude was friendly, a change she found both agreeable and unnerving.

Ever since he had returned from London yesterday the earl had been the soul of civil propriety. He had asked after her and Melissa's health with great solicitousness and had even gone so far as to suggest they drive out with him and see the estate. Although Melissa had declined with an uncomfortable look at him, Caroline had accepted with alacrity.

She admitted, as she flicked another sideways glance at Lord Devlon, that her reasons for coming had not been prompted by any overwhelming desire to see the estate. They had largely sprung from a wish to discover what had effected such a change in the earl over such a short period of time.

"In that rocky cove down there," he gestured toward the cliff's edge, which bounded one side of the road, "is a beach that can be reached only at low tide. It was used by brandy smugglers in the eighteenth century. Those lonely clumps of trees," he pointed a long hand toward a grove, "were planted on the horizon as landmarks for the boats."

"Really?" She affected an interest in the trees.

"Yes. It was quite a prospering business not so very long ago. I rather fancy some of the inhabitants of Hollowsby were a party to it." He continued with a grin, "There is nothing in the family history to suggest any of my august ancestors ever took part in smuggling, but I daresay they did. It was a lifeline along the coast and we have been a coastal family for generations."

"Yes," Caroline noted, smoothing the folds of her pale yellow muslin frock and assuming a deceptively demure attitude as she said wickedly, "There is a Devlon coat of arms above the fireplace in the purple bedroom. It has three creatures on it that look remarkably like rats descending a ship."

"They are ermine, Miss Norton," Lord Devlon replied with dignity. "They are leaving the ship of state to venture into the world."

"Indeed." Impishly she added, "They looked for all the world like rats jumping off a sinking boat."

Lord Devlon turned his face away from her but made no reply.

"I'm sorry, my lord. I shouldn't have said that," Caroline apologized. The unrepentance in her voice stole the sincerity from her words and her eyes sparkled merrily.

"Pray don't beg my forgiveness, Miss Norton. I am persuaded you have been waiting days for the opportunity to insert that piece of impertinence into your conversation with me. Well, consider it said. It's given me a very nice set-down."

Caroline ventured another sideways glance at the earl. The road twisted away from the cliff into a copse of trees and in the half-gloom of the shady oaks it was difficult to read his expression. But as they drove out into the sunlight again, she detected a slight twitch at the corner of his mouth.

"You thought that was diverting!" she accused in surprise.

"True," he acknowledged equably, never taking his eyes off the road, "but I didn't wish you to see my appreciation. I fancy you believe me to be bigheaded and you wished to say something to mill me down. Had I laughed at your words, it would have deprived you of that satisfaction."

"I *did* wish to give you a set-down," Caroline admitted candidly, and then allowed generously, as she primly crossed her hands on her lap and looked down at her yellow gown, "I don't think you precisely bigheaded, my lord."

"No? Odd, that. Men as conversable and charming as I am usually are."

The wealth of suppressed mirth twinkling in his eyes left her speechless for a moment. Recovering herself, she looked ahead and rejoined lightly. "Touché, my lord."

While Lord Devlon guided the horses through a particularly winding stretch of road Caroline tried to puzzle out the enigma of him. What had occurred to make the cold, dignified earl an amusing companion who not only traded light comments with her, but didn't even take offense at her saucy remarks? She felt certain they were statements that would have set his back up not a week earlier. What then, had happened to change him?

Pursuing these thoughts, she feigned casualness as she pulled her white cashmere shawl up on her shoulders. "You are in tolerably good spirits this morning. I do not recall your being so amiable before you left for London."

"It was an enlightening trip," he said ambiguously and then smoothly turned the conversation to matters outside himself.

As he continued his description of the estate, she quietly studied the man beside her. Lord Devlon held himself with the air of a man completely in control of himself and his surroundings. It was that attitude that set him apart from the other *ton* men she had known. As a group, she felt they could best be classified as gamesters, fops, and fools. Whatever else she could say about the earl, none of those words applied to him.

Caroline started in surprise when she realized he had addressed a question to her and was looking at her expectantly. "I beg your pardon," she said, flustered. "I didn't hear the question."

He smiled. "It doesn't signify."

She turned quickly away from him to study the countryside. It was odd how a man's smile could change his whole countenance so completely. His lips parted to reveal even white teeth, and the little crinkles next to his eyes wrinkled in an appealing way. He could really be quite charming, she considered. Caroline straightened in the seat; she must not let her imagination get completely away from her, painting the earl to be something other than what he really was. It would not do to romanticize a man who was doubtless only being kind now as part of an overall scheme against her niece. She must be ever on her guard against any warm and friendly feelings toward him.

The earl interrupted the silence between them to say, "One of the tenant's cottages is just around the bend. If you don't object, I would like to stop for just a moment."

They had passed the section of the coastline where chalk cliffs ended abruptly at the sea's edge. Now as they rounded a bend in the road, Caroline could see the flat, pebbly beach stretched out before them. It reminded her of the time she had spent some days at Chesil, not far from here, one summer when she was a child. Every day she and Georgiana and their mother had gone walking along the beach near the Fleet, the brackish lagoon separated by a natural seawall from the rest of the ocean.

Caroline looked away from the water as she realized they had stopped beside a cottage. Lord Devlon helped her alight, and they walked to the cottage door. There was no answer to his knock. In fact, the building looked deserted; no animals scurried around the overgrown yard to indicate otherwise.

"It appears no one lives here any longer," the earl said. "I was not aware it was unoccupied."

Caroline said nothing. Her eyes had once again gone to the sea. It was a sparkling deep blue and the small rounded pebbles on the beach made her long to take her shoes off and run through them as she had as a child. She immediately put that thought from her mind. What would Lord Devlon think of such an action?

"Would you mind if I look about?" he asked. "I should like to see what condition some of the buildings are in."

"Of course." On an impulse, she said casually, "I think I shall just walk down by the beach."

He nodded and started off toward a large stone barn. Caroline walked in the opposite direction, her steps quickening as she approached the water's edge. She smelled the salty sea air and listened to the sound of the gently lapping waves. At the water's edge she halted and looked back to see if the earl was in sight. When she did not spy him she hastily bent to touch the water. It was cool and inviting and again she longed to toss her shoes aside and wander barefooted into it.

Caroline started walking slowly along the edge of the water. The pebbles made delicate crunching noises under her feet as she walked. Stopping, she gazed out across the blue water, looking into the distance before her eyes moved slowly inward. She saw a mackerel swimming past before something glinting gold caught her attention. The tiny object was only a few feet out in the water, but she could not reach it from where she stood. She recalled with a smile how she and Georgiana had searched for gold from Spanish galleons every day they had been at Chesil. They had not found any, but they had never stopped looking.

She bent forward to peer at the glinting fragment. Gold? Caroline straightened and looked back toward the buildings. The earl was still not in sight. Without another hesitation she shed her shoes and lifted her skirts above her ankles. She tested the water with her toe delicately poised over the water's surface and drew back with a laughing shriek. It was cold! But treasures were to be had only by the daring. Still smiling happily, she raised her skirts an inch higher and started into the water.

Caroline was blithely unaware that she was being watched. Lord Devlon had turned sharply to look out the barn window at the sound of a woman's cry. He had been surprised at what he saw. Miss Norton, her skirts pulled up to display a dainty foot, was wading into the water with a childlike abandon, bending to look at something and then tossing it into the air with a laugh that carried back to him faintly. He watched with a bemused expression.

She skipped through the water and bent again, picked up another object, and carefully pocketed this one. Then she was off searching again. A grin spread across his face. Caroline Norton looked very happy and carefree picking up what he supposed were shells and pretty pebbles. He would not have thought her capable of such simple merriment.

As she moved through the cold water Caroline was smiling and humming to herself. She had not yet found any Spanish gold, but she had discovered two colorful rocks that might well be emeralds or some other precious gemstones, and she had tucked them reverently in the pocket of her sprigged muslin gown. She splashed farther through the water along the edge of the beach toward something else shining a few feet away. Caroline had completely forgotten Lord Devlon and even that she had come with him. For the moment she would not have been surprised to see her mother and Georgiana coming toward her with their white aprons held out in front of them, full of their finds from the sea. She bent to pick up another pretty rock while she continued to hold up her skirts with her other hand.

"Here is one you did not see."

At the sound of a man's voice Caroline started and turned in astonishment. A slow blush spread across her face when she saw Lord Devlon. "Oh," she murmured. "Oh, dear. I quite forgot myself."

"That's quite all right. Here, I've found a red pebble for you."

She walked up onto the beach and took it wordlessly. Suddenly she was aware that she was exposing a provocative view of her ankles, and she dropped the skirt hastily. "I do beg your pardon." What would he think of her wading around like this? "I must get my shoes," she said, avoiding his eyes.

"I took the liberty of bringing them." He extended her kid slippers with his other hand.

She raised her eyes to meet his and discovered they were brimming with laughter. Well, it *was* rather amusing, she considered as a smile crossed her face. She stretched out a hand to receive her shoes, still smiling. "Since I am so lost to decorum as to frolic in the water, I daresay you will not object if I sit on the beach and put my slippers on?"

"No, please be seated," he urged and then sat down beside her. "You are fond of the ocean?"

"Yes. I have spent but little time near it. My mother brought my sister and I to Chesil once to visit a friend," she explained. She put her second slipper on and then looked toward the earl. Encouraged by his open smile, she confided with a girlish giggle, "I fancied myself quite seaworthy at the time and meant to seek my fortune on the high seas with a band of pirates. I was seven at the time and, as I recall, it seemed a perfectly proper employment."

"Indeed." He picked up a pebble and tossed it out into the waves and watched to see how far it went. "What were you searching for just now?"

"Spanish gold," she answered with an artless laugh. "I didn't find any."

He tossed another pebble into the water. This one went farther, but he scarcely noticed. He had turned back toward his companion. The little wisps of hair around the edges of her purple bonnet were beginning to curl tighter in the dampness of the ocean air, the hem of her printed gown was wet as were her shoes, and her face was pink from her exercise. She looked thoroughly charming.

Caroline saw the earl look at her and realized how disheveled she must appear. But he didn't seem to be taking it in bad part. "I fear you must think me a hoyden. I pray you will not judge me too severely."

"I am pleased you have enjoyed yourself," he answered quickly. As for judging her too severely, he believed he already had. Any woman who could act so innocently playful could not be totally deceptive. Had he misjudged her? What if she had been a companion and wished to conceal the fact? Who of those who had come down in the world wished it known, if they could save themselves the embarrassment? As to that, being a companion was honest employment. Certainly it was preferable to being a pirate, he thought with a wry smile.

Caroline gathered up her skirts and began to rise. The earl stood quickly and helped her. "Thank you," she said. He left his hand on her elbow as they walked back to the curricle.

As he helped her into the vehicle he considered how pretty she looked. Although he had never been particularly partial to red hair, it suited Miss Norton quite well. Not that her hair was really red; it was more a pleasing color of burnished russet. Looking at her now, he decided it was the perfect shade for her, with her hazel eyes and the pale peach of her cheeks. She was an attractive enough chit on the surface. It was only her honesty that was suspect, he reminded himself morosely.

He forgot from time to time about the treasures that were missing. But the fact remained that they had begun to disappear on the day she had arrived. Still, nothing was proven. He pushed the disagreeable thoughts from his mind. It was proving to be a most enjoyable day and he had no wish to ruin it.

They started off down the road in companionable silence. "Tell me more about the estate and the conversable, modest gentlemen born at Hollowsby," Caroline said lightly.

"You mistake me, Miss Norton. We have boasted no births except those of babes at Hollowsby. Although," he noted with a gleam in his blue eyes, "I don't doubt there was a time you thought I must have sprung full-blown from the head of some devil."

"Well, *I* never thought that," Caroline said, "but Annie, of course, thought you *were* the devil when we first met you. After all, you did look rather frightening with your brow all black and thunderous and your greatcoat blowing back as you stalked into the room."

"I daresay she hasn't changed her mind."

"No, I fear not," Caroline admitted. "Annie is a bit stubborn in her ways. And if you wish to say it is a propensity that I share, you have my permission to say so, my lord," Caroline allowed handsomely.

"I should not dream of accusing you of being stubborn, Miss Norton," Lord Devlon replied gallantly, and then wisely turned the discussion to another subject. "Is the dog still in enforced confinement?"

Caroline nodded. "Yes. As a matter of fact, he has disgraced himself even further. This morning he sneaked into the kitchen and gobbled up an entire ragout of mutton before he was apprehended. A terrible thing," she clucked.

"Yes, but don't worry, your niece can get another dog if he dies."

She laughed. "He did take risks with his health to eat anything prepared in that kitchen," she admitted.

"It is a great pity the house has fallen into such a state," he said and then continued, looking off in the distance and seeming to forget she was present: "I can remember when I was but a child, people of the first consequence came to the lavish balls my mother gave. They drove up in fine carriages with elegant crests and alighted to be met by proper footmen. Except, perhaps for the intractable Frederick," he chuckled, and then continued seriously, "The interior of the house was vastly different from now. All of the furnishings were well maintained, and the hangings on every window were clean and new and added beauty to the room. When the house was aglow with the blaze of a thousand candles and the dancing continued into the small hours of the morning, I used to sit in my bedroom and think how very grand a house I lived in and—" Lord Devlon stopped short. "I beg your pardon," he said stiffly. "I did not mean to run on about something that can be of no interest to you."

"Oh, but I assure you, it is," Caroline replied. "I wish you will tell me more."

"You are very polite, but I know you cannot wish to be bored with stories of my past." He dismissed her request. "Have I shown you the old moat on the northern edge of the property?"

"No, you have not."

"I am certain you will be most interested in it," he said as he turned his attention back to the horses.

She nodded mutely. She wished the earl had not stopped when he had. It was obvious he had deep feelings for the house and property where he had spent his youth.

This was a different Lord Devlon. Or perhaps this was the first true glimpse she had had of him. Caroline had never really considered his side of their dispute before, but if he was so attached to his family home, she could understand why he wished to retain it. It was possible he really believed his brother had never been married to Melissa. Of course that was totally wrong, but it would explain his actions somewhat. The sensitivity he had shown today gave her food for thought.

CHAPTER 11

Caroline laid aside the book she had been trying to read and stared at the garden around her. But her mind was not occupied with the day lilies growing out of their borders or the other garden flowers creeping out of their beds to grow in a tangle about her, aided by the lack of pruning and gardening that prevailed at Hollowsby. What Caroline was considering as she chewed her lower lip thoughtfully, was Lord Devlon.

Since the day she had ridden with him over a week ago he had made no mention of their leaving or the missing heirlooms. Indeed, he had been courteous at all times, never giving the least hint that she and her niece were not the most honored of guests. Certainly he did not betray by word or deed that he found them troublesome, a fact he had been at no pains to hide when he had first arrived.

It was not a new subject of thought for Caroline. She had wondered over the earl's changed behavior since his return, but her efforts to discuss his transformation with Melissa had come to naught. Her niece was so glad to be on better terms with Lord

Devlon that she obviously did not wish to delve into the motive behind his metamorphosis.

"What are ye doin', ye simple woman?" a man's angry voice demanded loudly from just behind her.

Caroline dropped her book and jumped up. Frederick, his white hair and beard shaking along with the rest of his round frame, was standing not two yards from her, glaring.

"I have every right to be in this garden if I wish," she gasped indignantly. "That you would have the effrontery to—"

"Not ye!" He dismissed Caroline impatiently. "I'm not talkin' to ye. It's this one 'ere I'm talkin' to."

Caroline looked down where he pointed. There, kneeling not five feet from the bench, was Annie. Caroline's eyes widened at the sight of her maid. She was dressed in an old cambric gown of fading brown and kneeling in the dirt of what once had been a flower bed, digging with a large spoon.

"Annie! Whatever are you doing?" Caroline demanded.

"I'm digging snails," the old woman replied with dignity. "If that addlepated chemist don't carry them, then I shall make my own paste to rid us of that vicious dog-witch."

"You're digging up snails with a spoon!" Caroline cried. "How revolting!"

"I certainly wouldn't dig them with my hands," Annie replied with asperity. "Don't worry, I shall see that the spoon is washed before it is returned to the kitchen," she offered largely.

"I feel quite ill," Caroline said weakly.

"I have the very cure for that," Annie said brightly, "but I shall have to see if I can find some—"

"Don't tell me!" Caroline urged. "I have the greatest suspicion I shouldn't wish to know."

"Ignorance is a miserable curse," Annie replied, fastidiously plucking another snail from the dirt.

"Aye," Frederick intoned dourly, "ye should know all about ignorance. And there's even worse in store for ye if ye don't get out of those flowers this minute."

Annie, never one to tempt fate, especially when it took the form of a large, ill-tempered man, rose reluctantly and looked at him haughtily. "I hope a witch puts a hex on your garden, and everything in it dies."

"Would that be includin' ye too?" Frederick asked unforgivably.

"I wish the pair of you would stop fighting," Caroline intervened in exasperation. "Annie, take those snails," she paused to shudder delicately, "away from here."

"Those who do good works are never appreciated," the tiny woman noted virtuously as she picked up her jar and strolled down the garden path, counting her catch aloud while Frederick followed after her.

Caroline settled herself back on the bench, but she did not return to her book. Instead she considered what she should suggest to Melissa as their next course of action. Since the earl was being so polite she was loath to bring up the subject of his leaving.

But if he remained, no matter how civil he acted, it could only mean he was pursuing methods to dispossess Melissa of the house. Caroline put a hand to her forehead and rubbed absently. It was all so confusing. Perhaps if she waited a day or so a solution would present itself. Satisfied with her decision, she picked up the book and began to read again.

After dinner that evening Melissa excused herself pleading a headache. Caroline watched her go and then turned back to the earl. She was conscious that she was alone with him in the drawing room. Not that there was anything improper in that. After all, she was four-and-twenty and he had not the least designs on her. Still, she felt suddenly rather shy. He was watching her with an intentness she found rather disconcerting. She put her sampler down and rose to leave.

"Perhaps you would care to take a turn about the garden," he suggested as he laid aside a book he had been idly leafing through and stood also.

"Thank you, but I think not. I was just preparing to retire," she explained. She tried to avoid looking at the ormolu clock, which proclaimed it was just past eight o'clock. No one retired at such an early hour unless they were ill.

"So soon?" Lord Devlon asked bluntly. "A breath of crisp country air would do you a world of good." With a meaningful smile he added, "And I promise to conduct myself as a gentleman while we are in the moonlit garden together."

"I know you would behave in a perfectly correct fashion," she said stiffly. But the idea of being with him in the garden seemed somehow more intimate than was wise.

"Good," he said before she had a chance to speak. Crossing the room to her, he offered his arm. Caroline hesitated and then extended her own. She would enjoy a short walk in the night air. The fact it would be with Lord Devlon, she had to own, made the thought even more appealing.

"Just a brief stroll," she murmured. "I really am tired," she added unconvincingly.

He led her through the musty house and out into the garden. By night its glaring defects were not so evident. In fact, the tangled garden seemed rather romantic with a fuzzy half-moon spreading a pale glow over it. In the uncertain light the earl looked even more darkly handsome than usual, she mused, then put the thought firmly aside.

They ambled peacefully down the silent paths for a few moments before he broke the stillness between them. "There is something I wish to say to you."

When he did not continue, she asked, "What is it, my lord?"

Lord Devlon drew in a breath of air. Even now, he considered, it wasn't necessary for him to speak of their leaving. Perhaps he ought not broach the subject for a day or so. After all, everything had been going quite nicely for the past few days, and there was no need for unseemly haste in removing the ladies from the house.

He glanced down at the woman beside him and met her curious look. Her eyes, he noticed, held a certain liveliness that he had remarked in them more often of late. And she was dressed in a cranberry gown, which set off her complexion to perfection. Her hair, too, had been dressed more stylishly recently. Today she had a white ribbon threaded through her bronze curls. He liked the effect. In fact, he knew a moment's desire to reach out his hand and touch one of her soft locks.

"Is something wrong with my hair?" she asked, raising her hand to it uncertainly as he continued to stare at her.

"No, of course not."

Caroline felt an unwonted disappointment that he had not followed his denial up with a compliment about her hair. Perhaps he had not noted that she had changed the style.

"Miss Norton," he began briskly—it probably wasn't wise to delay this matter any longer, as he was showing the most alarming interest in this woman in spite of all the good reasons why he should not. "I will state my case plainly. I am willing to concede that your niece owns Hollowsby. However, I would ask a favor of you."

"And what is that, my lord?" The introduction of business into their leisurely walk through the overgrown but quaint garden annoyed Caroline. She found herself wondering crossly why he had to discuss a subject that was bound to bring them to cross swords again.

"As you know," he continued, "I wish to retain my family home. I am willing to give Miss Courtney an estate in Leicestershire that is in far better condition than this. One," he added with a smile, "that comes complete with meek, biddable servants."

"I am grown rather used to Frederick's recalcitrance," Caroline noted, looking toward a cluster of low-hanging dogwood trees and pretending not to realize the earl was watching her with a quizzical expression.

"You could go to my estate in Leicestershire and make certain you were not being offered something unacceptable. Although," he looked about the overgrown garden and continued, "you have my word it is a great deal better tended than Hollowsby."

"Then why do you want Hollowsby?" she asked bluntly. "Is there buried treasure here?"

"Only Clover's bones," he replied, stopping in front of a lichen-covered statue and gazing at it. "But it is my family home. I wish to return it to its original glory."

"I had not thought you such a romantic, my lord," she replied tartly.

"Ah, I see you do not trust me." He gave a light laugh. "The Devlons are not an entirely unscrupulous lot, Miss Norton. I assure you, what I offer is worth much more than what your niece will have if she chooses to remain here."

Caroline turned and faced him squarely. "But if she does choose to remain here, you would not continue to contest the marriage?"

"I should dislike losing Hollowsby." He paused. "No," he shook his head slowly, "I wouldn't contest her claim. If she wishes to stay, then I shall abide by that wish."

"You are become very generous, my lord. Or," she continued thoughtfully, "you have realized you have no choice. After all, this land was left to Melissa by your brother, and you cannot reverse the actions of those who are dead, as much as you might like to."

He bowed. "You have no idea how much I wish I could reverse Chester's actions." Lord Devlon regarded Caroline with an unreadable expression, his blue eyes betraying none of his thoughts. He continued slowly. "As you say, I cannot change the past. Therefore, I shall attempt to do the best I can. Will you accept my offer?"

CHAPTER 12

All in all, Lord Devlon considered as he lounged in front of a low burning fire in the study, he was handling things quite well. Miss Norton and her niece had been disposed of honorably, or soon would be, and he had what he wanted most, Hollowsby. Or he very nearly had it, which was the same thing. Once Melissa saw the estate in Leicestershire, she would not consider coming back to this ramshackle house. Then he would be free to turn his attention to the very real task of making it a suitable place to live.

Of course he still intended to spend most of his time in London. After all, that was where the better part of his friends were, and his friends with better parts, he considered with a lazy smile at the thought of a certain young opera singer. He had neglected his social life far too long, rusticating here in Dorset, but that would all be over shortly.

It was a bit of a pity, he considered, reclining further back in the Windsor chair and absently studying the high gloss of his boots, that he would not be seeing more of Miss Norton. Although she was not at all his style of woman—he preferred them more docile than she could ever aspire to be—there was something about her that he nevertheless found appealing. But there were women anxious to attract his interest wherever he went, so it hardly signified if he did not see her again.

With these matters concluded to his satisfaction, Lord Devlon rose and walked toward the music room. He fancied he had seen Caroline—Miss Norton, he corrected himself—there before he had retired to the study to answer some correspondence. He might as well go along and see what she was doing. After all, it was his duty as host to see that his guests were entertained.

Stopping at the door of the music room, he watched Caroline pounding out a lusty, if ill-played, tune. Her auburn curls had tumbled down out of their dark riband and framed her face in carefree abandon. Her gown, a pretty peach gauze over a white material, was scooped low across her bosom. As she bent toward the keys, she unconsciously afforded the earl a tantalizing view. Melissa was seated in a needlepoint chair beside her aunt, turning pages and humming along absurdly off-key. Asleep on the floor was Clover, snoring against the raucous beat.

Caroline banged out the closing notes of the tune and turned toward her niece with a hearty laugh. "We are positively beyond hope."

"Clover likes it well enough," Melissa objected. "It was so soothing, he went to sleep listening to it."

"I am most flattered," Caroline responded lightly. She looked up in surprise as Lord Devlon walked toward them. "I did not see you enter, my lord. I hope you have not heard the whole of that dreadful piece." A blush of embarrassment stained her cheeks. "If you are a music lover, I fear you have come to the wrong room."

"Nonsense. Music has charms to soothe the savage breast."

"Yes," Caroline nodded toward Clover, "as you can see." She closed the lid of the pianoforte and began to put the music sheets in a neat stack, intent on busying herself to avoid Lord Devlon's eyes.

"Don't quit on my account," he protested. He stopped beside a large old harp and idly ran a finger across it. "I like watching you play. It tells me something about you to see the determination with which you approach it."

"It tells you I can't play," Caroline quipped, rising and making a wide path around her slumbering adversary.

"I disagree. But if you won't perform, at least sit and talk with me." He gestured toward a loveseat.

Instead she seated herself on a chair across from it. Smoothing the folds of her gown with care, she kept her eyes demurely downcast. When she glanced up, the earl was watching her with a bemused expression. She said hurriedly, "I have spoken with Melissa, my lord, about your offer." She turned to her niece. "My dear, why do you not come here and explain to his lordship what we have decided?"

The younger woman stood hastily and roused Clover. "It is just time for Clover's walk, Auntie Caro.

Can you not explain to Lord Devlon what we concluded?"

Caroline repressed a sigh of exasperation and turned back to the earl with a helpless look while Melissa left the room with Clover trudging sleepily after her.

"Why is it that I have this unshakable feeling your niece does not wish to speak to me?" he asked with a disarming smile as he settled himself onto the loveseat.

"She is very young, my lord. And you can be most forbidding. I fear she is foolishly in awe of you."

"And you are not," he noted with a wry grin.

"No," she admitted, "but then I am very much more used to men than she is."

"Indeed?" he asked with a slight lift of one dark eyebrow.

Why she should feel so disconcerted by the earl's gaze escaped Caroline. All she knew was that she did. "That is not the matter at hand," she said swiftly. "Melissa and I have decided to accept your offer to repair to Leicestershire. In fact, we will leave in the morning, if that is acceptable to you."

Lord Devlon did not reply for a moment. His eyes lingered on her face. With her cheeks still pink from her fading blush and her hazel eyes wide and sparkling, she looked compellingly fragile. Leave in the morning? Well, damn, of course it was agreeable with him. Why did he feel dejected at the knowledge they were departing so soon?

"Is tomorrow all right, my lord?" Caroline asked again.

"Oh, indeed, entirely so."

"Very well. If it is not too much trouble, I think we should leave Clover here for the time being. If Melissa likes Leicestershire and decides to remove there permanently, she can have the remainder of her things sent and Clover could come at that time."

"You have my assurances no harm will come to him while you are gone," he declared solemnly.

"I'd as lief have your word Clover would vanish mysteriously," she laughed and then added wickedly, "going the way of the other valuable pieces."

He turned the talk away from that quagmire of conversation with a light question. "Is your maid still looking for the cure to rid the house of him?"

"When last I saw Annie," Caroline confided, "she was trying to tempt him to eat the snail paste she had concocted and having precious little success, I might add. Clover's diet does not run to snails, I fear."

"The animal is smarter than I gave him credit for being."

"I doubt that. And now, my lord," she stood quickly, suddenly aware that they had drifted into a companionable conversation and embarrassed by that knowledge, "if you will excuse me, I must see to the packing. I need to locate Frederick to open a chest of drawers in my room that is stuck."

"Permit me to assist you, Miss Norton," he said, rising politely.

"Don't be ridiculous. It is a servant's job." Caroline objected.

"If all the deeds that fall under that title were performed by those admirable persons, I am persuaded the house would not be in such a shocking state of disrepair," he noted dryly. "Besides, I doubt you could find Frederick. I have yet to establish the precise position he occupies—be it butler, footman, or gardener. But he was a nefarious servant at best even when I was a jam-faced urchin and now he has become even worse and is rarely available when needed."

"Well, *his* position may be in doubt, but yours is not. You are an earl and entirely above opening drawers in ladies' bedrooms."

Lord Devlon suppressed a devilish grin. Miss Norton would have been most surprised if she knew how many drawers he had opened in just such bedrooms. But he merely offered his hand to her. "You needn't worry about the impropriety of my being in your room, you know. We have only to leave the door open. Or, better yet, we could summon Clover as a chaperon. I doubt that anything in the least objectionable would occur with him pacing and growling."

"Clover won't be necessary," Caroline said crisply.

They walked into the rotunda and up the marble staircase. As Caroline mounted the steps beside the earl she felt suddenly rather shy and searched for something witty and sophisticated to say that would return her to her usual confidence. But nothing came to mind as they continued wordlessly to her room.

Lord Devlon stood back to permit her to enter and then stepped in behind her, scrupulously leaving the door ajar.

Caroline pointed to a highboy in the corner that was adorned with richly carved cabrioles. "It is the bottom one, my lord."

She turned back to the earl to discover he was standing close to her, very close, and making no move toward the highboy. "Oh," she said faintly as he reached out a long hand and pushed an errant curl from her face. They stared at each other wordlessly before their heads moved, one bending and one tilting upward, and their lips finally touched.

Caroline had been kissed before, but she did not recall any that were so gratifying, that made her feel happy from her toes to the tip of her head. And none that had inspired such awe. But as his lips moved across hers with a lightness made all the more delightful because she could feel the restrained masculinity behind them, she felt a blissful resignation.

Reality edged back in as he drew back from her and surveyed her with approval.

"I'm sure we should not have done that," she whispered.

The catch in her voice was so appealing that Lord Devlon was tempted to repeat the offense.

"I mean," she looked away, flustered, "it is really too bad."

"Bad? I thought it quite good," he teased, "but if you think we are in want of practice, I will be glad to oblige."

"We are alone in a bedroom!" she cried, backing away a step. "This simply isn't done!"

Lord Devlon, who could have pointed out that a great deal of kissing took place in a great number of bedrooms, did not pursue the argument. He was, rather, engrossed in explaining his actions to himself. Why he had kissed Miss Norton he could not entirely say. But she was absolutely right. He should not be dallying in her bedroom. In fact, he should open the drawer and leave while he still possessed his full senses. And they were something in doubt now if he must force his attentions on unemployed companions.

"The bottom one?" he asked brusquely.

Caroline looked at him, startled by his sudden change in mood, and nodded mutely.

Lord Devlon knelt to the drawer and began to work at it, pressing in on one side while he pushed out on the other. "It was always hard to open," he said, straining at it as he spoke. "I see it has become more so with the years." He gave one final heave and the drawer flew open with an unexpectedness that sent him backward. With it, the drawer above also slid open, revealing its contents: small vases, statues, jeweled swords and cups.

Lord Devlon blinked as if he were seeing a ghost. Slowly, he rose and faced Caroline. "What are these, Miss Norton?" His voice was toneless, but his face had taken on the same thunderous aspect she had noted at their first meeting.

Caroline ventured a step closer, wary of the look on Lord Devlon's face, and peered into the drawer. "I don't know what they are," she replied in confusion.

"I fancy I can enlighten you," he returned sarcastically. "The objects that grace your drawer are quite lovely. Pity they cannot be on display. But then one of the servants might discover them."

"What are you talking about?" she demanded.

He passed a look of contempt over her upturned face. "These, Miss Norton, are the family treasures that have been missing since your arrival. The ones about which you knew nothing," he added sardonically.

"I didn't know they were there!"

"Come, Miss Norton, surely you do not intend to try to flummery me with such a simple tale as that?"

"I am not trying to flummery you!"

"No, I daresay you are not or you should have come up with a likelier story than that rather dull-witted one." Lord Devlon's anger was rising even as he spoke. And the look of pure innocence on Caroline's face was kindling it to even greater heights. "You needn't look so shocked. It is obvious you are caught out, so you might as well confess."

Caroline drew herself up with dignity. "You may believe what you wish, my lord. I give you full leave to think me a thief and a liar to boot. But I maintain I knew nothing of this." She waved an unsteady hand at the heap of valuables leering at her from the drawer.

"I thank you for your permission to call you what I have deduced you are," he snapped. "Is this all? Or have you already smuggled some out of the house and sold them?" His voice rose in volume and he moved toward her.

She retreated a step, then caught herself and stood firm. "If you will but listen, you will see that I am telling the truth. Surely you must realize I would never keep such objects in my room if I had stolen them. Someone else has obviously put them here."

"Obviously," he echoed sarcastically.

"Saints preserve us! What's all the screeching about?" Annie demanded as she rushed into the room, looking wildly around and holding a broom poised ready to strike. "Is it Clover again?"

"You may put that down," Lord Devlon commanded sternly. "The problem here is not a dog, but a thief."

Caroline gasped. "How dare you accuse me of stealing in front of a servant? You have no basis to make such a claim."

Annie ventured closer, lowering the broom reluctantly and letting it trail after her to the floor. "Stealing? What's been taken?"

"These." He swept a hand toward the drawer. "Do you know anything about them?"

"No," she replied, speechless with amazement for a space of ten seconds. Then she recovered her tongue and turned her wrinkled face toward the earl and suggested, "Perhaps a witch put a hex on her and made her do it."

"I think not," he growled. "Miss Norton," he turned back to Caroline with bored deference, "if you would be so good as to adjourn to the study, we can discuss this matter where we won't be interrupted by servants, since you are so very fine and particular in your manners."

She nodded coldly and walked stiffly down the steps in front of him.

Once inside the study, he slammed the door behind her with a resounding force. "Now, Miss Norton, sit down and I shall tell you what is to be done."

"I—"

"Do not interrupt me," he thundered. "I have been patient long enough."

Caroline jumped at the sound of his voice but subsided into the Windsor chair when he gestured peremptorily. He continued angrily. "I will not allow you or your niece to remain here. I will not house an ungrateful thief!"

"Will you house a grateful one, my lord?" Caroline shouted, her anger matching his own.

He continued imperiously. "I need no longer let my scruples as a gentleman interfere with my wishes. I suggest you take advantage of my generous nature and leave before I change my mind and take legal action against you."

Caroline's already white face blanched even further. "If you think for one instant—"

"Silence!" His word cracked through the room like a loud and unexpected clap of thunder. "There is more to this macabre tale than even you may know. Since you choose not to act with honor, I think I can safely forsake mine enough to tell you that your niece was never married to my brother. There was no record of the wedding at St. George's. If you will but ask your niece, you will discover she was 'married' by a man who lives at Mannly Wood off the Exeter road. In short, Miss Norton, my brother was living with the child out of wedlock."

"That," he said, stalking about the room angrily,

"is why I have been at such pains with you and the girl of late. I realize my brother behaved with shocking want of propriety and I was willing to let the matter pass. I intended to give her a handsome estate and all the money she needed and let the whole matter die. But even while I was thinking how to spare pain to your family, you were sneaking about my house stealing from beneath my nose. I'll not let anyone use me that way!"

The icy contempt in Lord Devlon's voice was equaled by the steely look radiating from his blue eyes. Caroline sat stunned, her mind struggling to assimilate the words he flung at her. But she had already come to an intuitive understanding that he spoke the truth. Melissa had no claim on the earl and certainly Caroline did not. The best thing left to do was to leave—immediately.

CHAPTER 13

Caroline found Melissa in the garden dressed in an old gray gown. Her hair was caught up in a bandeau of parchment-colored silk, but rebellious blonde curls escaped from it to dance about her forehead. Melissa was oblivious to her appearance as she bent over a large wooden tub, intent on giving Clover a bath.

"Pack your things," Caroline began by way of greeting. "We are leaving immediately."

"I thought we were not going to Leicestershire until tomorrow," Melissa said, rising and looking at her aunt in confusion as she shook the water from her hands.

"We are not going there at all," Caroline returned. "We are removing to Wiltshire. From there you will go to Ireland to your mother."

"But what about Leicestershire?" Melissa struggled to comprehend this drastic change in plans as she pushed back wet tendrils from her face with the back of her hand. "Aren't we going there? Isn't Lord Devlon giving it to us in exchange for leaving Hollowsby?"

"In return for our leaving Hollowsby, I believe his lordship is willing not to press charges against me. Although," Caroline said darkly, "I am not altogether certain of that. He was in quite a royal dudgeon when I left him."

"He was?" Melissa asked blankly. "But I thought we were doing what he wanted. I mean, didn't he wish us to go to another estate?"

Caroline sank onto a wooden bench with a defeated look and regarded Clover morosely. "Yes," she sighed. "That was what he had originally wanted. But something terrible has happened in the meantime. The missing family treasures have been found in my room. Lord Devlon was nearly beside himself with rage and has ordered us from the house."

"Did he accuse you of stealing them?" Melissa demanded in astonishment.

"Yes. The fool!" Caroline expostulated. "If I had been dull-witted enough to take the trinkets, I would hardly have hidden them in a drawer in my own room and then asked him to open another drawer in that same bureau. But his lordship was not of an opinion to consider that as evidence of my innocence. At any rate," she clasped her hands before her and shook her head, "it does not matter whether I took the baubles or not. In his anger, Lord Devlon revealed something that is far more serious than any paltry theft."

"What?" Melissa wiped her hands on her gown and seated herself beside Caroline. Clover sat back in the tub and regarded both women with a questioning look.

Melissa's aunt gazed at her regretfully. Pushing back a lock of Melissa's blonde hair, Caroline felt her anger begin to disperse. There was no need to be cruelly blunt; Melissa was such a trusting child. How could Caroline tell her that she had been tricked by the man she had believed herself married to? With another sigh Caroline resigned herself to the lamentable fact that if she did not tell her niece, Lord Devlon very well might. And he would do so in far less kindly terms than she would use.

"Melissa, when you and Chester were married, well, the ceremony was—" She broke off, searching for the right word.

Melissa looked at her curiously. "It was a lovely ceremony, Auntie Caro. There were blue forget-me-nots and some lovely white flowers. I'm not sure what kind they were, but they smelled quite nice. And the bishop was such a kind man. He kept pinching my arm and saying what a prime handful I was. And then he'd laugh and wink at Chester. It was ever so charming." She smiled dreamily at the memory.

Caroline tried again. "Did it not appear peculiar for a bishop to behave in such a forward manner? Did it never occur to you that he might not be a bishop at all?"

"Oh, I know that," Melissa assured her with a giggle. "After we left his house, Chester laughed about him in the carriage and said he was the veriest schemer. Chester said he had never been anything more than a vicar—and a very dishonest one who robbed the church boxes for his own use—but it increased his consequence to be called a bishop."

Caroline sighed. Chester, rest his soul, sounded like a very plausible scoundrel himself. Certainly he must have been capable of throwing about the most outrageous lies without the merest blink of an eye. Well, she was going to have to disillusion Melissa sooner or later. Taking a deep breath, she pursued, "The bishop was not the only one pretending to be something he wasn't. Chester was not entirely honest with you."

"He wasn't an earl?" Her niece's green eyes grew round with disbelief.

"He was an earl," Caroline assured her, "but he wasn't a gentleman." She stood and paced in frustration. "He did not marry you. He hired someone to play the role of clergyman to make you think you were married."

Melissa looked stunned. "Why did he do that? I told him I would marry him. And he left me Hollowsby, so he must have liked me."

"He liked you," Caroline said gently, "but he needed your mother's permission to marry you. Apparently she was not to be found at the time so he decided to just—" She broke off unhappily. What could she say to make something sound right that hadn't been? But she couldn't allow her niece to go on believing she had been lawfully wed. "At any rate, the point is that Chester willed you Hollowsby as his wife. Since you were never his wife, you do not own it, or anything else of his."

"Not even Clover?" Melissa pressed in horror.

Caroline passed a hand across her face and prayed for patience. "Yes, I daresay you do own Clover. I am persuaded Lord Devlon will not object if you take him." She privately thought it would serve the earl well if Clover was left behind, but she said nothing on that head. "That hardly signifies right now. Do you not see we must leave and do so immediately? We are trespassers on Lord Devlon's land and I don't wish to be beholden to him for anything whatsoever. We shall return to Wiltshire and then you can proceed to Ireland."

"But Mama won't know I'm coming. She might not want me there."

"There is no other choice, Melissa," Caroline rejoined impatiently. "Now, we must leave."

Melissa nodded and rose slowly. "I shall be ready shortly," she assured Caroline as she turned toward the house.

"Good."

Seeing his mistress leave, Clover must have realized his bath had come to an end. Before Caroline knew what he was about, he stepped out of the wooden tub, gave a short bark of warning, and then dried himself in one great shake that left Caroline uncomfortably wet.

"I should have expected that," she muttered to herself as she gave the dog a blighting look and turned toward the house. Inside, she summoned Annie and announced tersely, "We must pack to return to Wiltshire."

"Why?" the old woman asked in surprise.

"I thought you wished to go back there," Caroline retorted. "You have done nothing but complain of the food since we arrived here."

"Well, I don't think it's worth a trip to Wiltshire just because I do not like the food," she noted practically. "It would be far more to the point to hire another cook."

Caroline clenched her teeth and explained. "Our visit here is at an end. Melissa and I will be going to Wiltshire."

"Just as well," the maid approved. "I don't like this house, and I don't like the earl above half. And so I told you the first time I saw him."

"Yes, I should have listened to your sage words. Now, if we have concluded our discussion, you may pack my clothes. After that, I wish you will help Melissa. We shall be gone as soon as may be."

Annie set about packing while Caroline crossed to the wardrobe, flung the door open, and grabbed the first dress she touched. Folding it carelessly, she tossed it onto the tester bed and plucked another from the press. This one she crumpled and let fall to the floor, abandoning packing altogether as she stalked toward the door. She had to get away from the house to sort out the thoughts churning wildly in her head.

"You're never going out like that?" Annie's words stopped her.

Caroline flicked a rueful glance down at her wet gown, then closed the door. No, she couldn't go like this. Even if the gown weren't cold and damp, it was clinging in a most revealing manner. And she had no wish to see the earl looking as she did now. In fact, she appended angrily, she had no wish to see him ever again. But certainly not dressed in this manner. It would only serve to support his low opinion of her.

It was, Caroline reflected as she turned back to the room, an opinion he had temporarily abandoned. For a time she had thought he held her in some regard. And when he kissed her, she had even wondered . . . She broke off and called sharply. "Annie! Do help me out of this wet gown!"

Her maid hastened to do as she was bid, her fingers working rapidly down the row of white onyx buttons. "You had best put on something warm," she advised. "You wouldn't wish to take a chill and be sick."

"I don't care if I do," Caroline replied with childish defiance.

Annie shrugged. "You'd have to stay here until you were well if you did."

Those words sent Caroline over to the wardrobe to pull out a heavy woolen navy gown. She slipped her wet garments off and donned the dry one hastily. Then she turned her attention to arranging the details of their departure. That task soon occupied her so completely that she pushed all thoughts of the earl to the back of her mind.

It was only when the luggage was safely stored atop the carriage and everyone was lined up to board that Caroline allowed herself a moment to think how she should best take her leave of Lord Devlon. After all, she didn't wish him to have the last word. Her pride revolted at such a thought. Why should she slink off like some servant who had been dismissed for stealing the family silver? She had not stolen the first thing, regardless of what appearances might indicate.

Galvanized into action by her remembrance of the earl's harsh words, Caroline turned to Melissa, who was endeavoring to coax Clover into the vehicle. "I wish to speak to his lordship. He has apparently forgotten to come to say good-bye to us. You may wait in the coach, it will only be a moment," she told Annie when her maid showed signs of following her.

"Yes, ma'am. But the dog. I didn't know he would be going with us. I really don't wish to ride with him and—"

Caroline cut through her objections. "Annie, Clover will sleep during the journey so you needn't worry. Once we arrive in Wiltshire, you need never see him again."

The older woman opened her mouth to make one more protest but Caroline's implacable look must have convinced her that the dog would be the course of least resistance after all. "Very well," she capitulated gracelessly.

Caroline marched up the steps of the house, through the rotunda toward the study. There she found Lord Devlon writing at his desk.

"We are leaving, my lord," she began haughtily. "I thank you for your kind hospitality."

He gave her a scathing look, but said nothing as he rose slowly from his desk in grudging acknowledgement of her sex.

"When you find the person responsible for stealing the bric-a-brac, I wish you would send me a note," she continued, ignoring his look. "I should be most interested to learn who it was."

"Is there anything else you wished to be apprised of?" Lord Devlon asked, his face set in a hard line that made his dark eyebrows look even more sinister and forbidding.

"No. You are welcome to look through our luggage for further valuables." Her voice held a cutting edge. "You have my assurance the only thing we are taking from the house is Clover. Of course, if you had rather we did not, you may discuss the matter with my niece, but she seems most determined to take him."

"She is welcome to him," he said shortly.

"You are *too* kind, my lord," Caroline said in a voice laden with sweet sarcasm.

"I know," he replied evenly.

She departed with a thin smile on her lips and a proud tilt to her head that was only marred by the fact that her hair was still damp from her encounter with Clover.

It was not until the carriage was a good five miles from Hollowsby that Caroline allowed herself to wonder why she had sought Lord Devlon out. Nothing had been served by her histronics, and he was doubtless thinking her an even greater fool for having paid a final call on him, given the circumstances.

She blinked resolutely at the film of moisture that invaded her eyes, caused, no doubt, by the dust of the road. It was at that inopportune moment that Clover, who was lying on the floor and who had grown more and more bleary-eyed as the trip progressed, relieved himself of his lunch with a sickening sound.

Caroline turned her face to look out the window while Melissa frantically pulled the check string, and the carriage was brought to a halt. The travelers descended to await the cleaning of the coach.

It was an unpromising beginning to a trip, but then, Caroline considered, it was entirely in keeping with the events of the rest of the day.

CHAPTER 14

"You met Rye Bythestone!" Trevina exclaimed. Her face lighted in an expression of incredulous delight. "You sly thing. You did not tell me he was Melissa's brother. How very fortunate for you."

"I did not know that Lord Devlon was any relation. In fact," Caroline continued crossly, "I had never heard of him before I went to Hollowsby."

"Not heard of him! How utterly ridiculous. That," she pronounced sagely, "is what comes of not reading the society pages of the *Gazette,* but instead burying yourself in books. For the past three Seasons he has been the talk of the town. He spent a little time in London before that or he should have been earlier."

"I don't doubt that. With his manners he was bound to be," Caroline said waspishly.

Trevina was paying no heed to her friend's words. She had jumped up from her seat in the red room and paced excitedly to the bow window, her face a wreath of happy smiles. "Did he take any particular note of you? Don't hesitate. You can tell me, dear Caroline." Trevina regarded her with a hopeful expression.

163

"He took most particular note of me," Caroline replied. She averted her eyes downward and twisted her handkerchief in her hands.

"Famous! Then he may call on you. Oh, my dear." Trevina fluttered back to seat herself on the gold Chippendale sofa beside Caroline. "You are not telling me the whole of it. Is there a romance? Yes, of course there is!" She answered her own question without waiting for a response. "How can there not be when a handsome man who is shockingly rich and a pretty woman spend time alone in the country? You had ample time to become acquainted. I am persuaded the results were explosive." She gurgled with delight.

"They were indeed," Caroline muttered. She set her teacup down and rose. "I believe I shall go upstairs and look in on Melissa. She will be leaving to go to her mother's tomorrow, so she won't be any trouble to you. Of course, she is a very quiet girl, so she shouldn't be the least inconvenience anyway."

Trevina blinked uncertainly. "Leaving? Why so soon? The child only just arrived today. Surely she wishes to rest a day or so before beginning another arduous journey."

"I think it would be better if she left the country with all due speed. She will be better situated with her mother in Ireland." And out of the range of gossip should Lord Devlon spread his tale about, she thought.

"Oh, but of course, the poor girl is but lately become a widow and wishes to be with her mother in her hour of need."

Caroline merely nodded. She didn't feel capable of explaining the whole of their departure from Hollowsby just yet, even to her friend. It disturbed the never-quite-slumbering ache in her chest to even think of the Dorset estate and the events that had taken place there. She had had ample time to review them in her mind on the trip back to Wiltshire. The one thing that caused her the most pain was the knowledge that the earl had tried to spare Melissa unhappiness by not telling them of his discovery that the marriage had not been legal. But, she reminded herself, he had been shielding his brother as well. It would have been kinder if he had told them the facts immediately. As it had turned out, it was even more humiliating to realize they had stayed at Hollowsby on his charity for eight extra days. Besides, whatever kindness he may have meant to show Melissa had been completely offset by the fact he had accused Caroline of stealing.

It was such a hopeless tangle. She ran a hand across her forehead and asked Trevina, "I wonder if Melissa might have the loan of a maid? She is without one at present; she was using Annie at Hollowsby."

"Of course. Annie can go with her to Ireland," Trevina offered largely. "She loves to travel."

"I think perhaps someone other than her might be better. She is but lately returned home." Caroline made a tactful attempt to grant the old woman a reprieve from any further time with Clover.

"Nonsense," Trevina laughed. "She loves to travel, and she has always wished to go to Ireland. She will like it above things. I shall tell her immediately." With those cheerful predictions Trevina bustled from the room to inform Annie of her new assignment.

Caroline walked wearily up the steps to Melissa's room in the wake of her friend's lavender skirts. She found her niece, looking forlorn and tear-streaked, on the edge of her carved, four-poster bed.

"I am sorry I did not come down to tea, Auntie Caro, but I am quite tired. You aren't angry with me, are you?"

"Of course not, dear." Caroline crossed the room and seated herself on the bed. "Is that why you are crying? I must own you have had it very hard of late. You have not even had the proper time to mourn your husb—Chester's death, and now you are burdened with additional problems."

Melissa sniffed and searched for a handkerchief in the voluminous pockets of her black taffeta dress. "It was terribly sad about Chester, but that is not why I am crying."

Caroline prodded. "Is it because his brother—"

"Oh no! It's—" She broke off to blow her nose lustily into the dainty scrap of lace before turning red-rimmed eyes to her aunt. "I don't know what to do about Clover. I don't wish to take him to Ireland with me. He travels very badly, and he is *quite* ill." At the thought of her pet's suffering, Melissa burst into a renewed flood of tears. "But there is no one to leave him with."

Caroline rose from the bed and walked to the window, looking at the well-tended garden below and then farther in the distance to where the fields stretched into the horizon. The noble thing for her to do would be to say she would keep Clover: Caroline knew that. But the thought of spending her remaining years with a dog like Clover went sorely against her grain.

"I don't think he would be happy with me," she said and then forced herself to add, "Of course, I would offer to take care of him otherwise. But I know he is attached to you. I'm persuaded he wishes to be with you."

Melissa rose hastily from the bed and declared soulfully, "Yes, and I wish to be with him. Only he is not well enough to travel as yet. Perhaps in a month's time he would be recovered and could make the journey. But he is most ill now and I feel dreadfully sorry for him." She ended on a pathetic note and paused to dash a tear from her eye.

As Caroline recalled the memory of Clover retching on the floor of the carriage, she shuddered delicately. Even she, in her hatred for the pestilent beast, had known a moment of pity as he had lain lifelessly in the vehicle. "I shall keep Clover until such time as he is able to go to Ireland," she promised, feeling the martyr.

"Oh, thank you! I shall remember this the rest of my life," Melissa assured her with fervent gratitude as she clasped Caroline's hands.

"At the very least," Caroline murmured. Thoughts of the ensuing days spent in the company of Clover crowded into her mind, making her feel quite ill.

Well, she considered, as she prepared for dinner later that evening, assisted by her own, now recovered, maid. At least the dog would offer her some means of occupying her time. She needed somewhere to channel her thoughts just now. The memories of the days spent at Hollowsby had crept into her brain with disturbing stubbornness during her journey back to Wiltshire, refusing to be banished.

And they continued to intrude as she tumbled into bed that night and closed her eyes. Lord Devlon, looking self-righteous and pitiless—the image of him was vivid in her mind—had ordered her from his house! Well, she didn't want his pity anyway, or anything else from him. She would never even think of him again, she resolved, turning over restlessly in the bed and thumping the pillow.

It was a resolution that proved not so easy to keep. Thoughts of Lord Devlon continued to flit around in her head, even after she fell asleep. He stalked through her dreams with his great coat billowing, his hair windswept and his blue eyes burning. As he stood before her making false accusation after false accusation, she thought with total irrelevancy how very handsome he looked in his dark, masculine way and how wonderful it had felt when he had kissed her.

They were pleasant enough fantasies in the night but not so agreeable to ponder the next morning. When Caroline arrived downstairs for breakfast, she had heavy circles under her eyes and a rather grim expression on her face.

Trevina looked at her in astonishment. "You look terrible," she greeted her.

"I endeavor to be worthy of all compliments," Caroline said stiffly, seating herself at the breakfast table and staring glumly at the plate.

"Don't be a goose. Tell me what is amiss. You look like you have been engaged in a fight and come off much the worst."

"I have and I did and I do not wish to discuss it," Caroline said with starched dignity. She immediately voided the effect of her words by slumping in her chair and moaning, "Oh, Trevina, I feel absolutely wretched! Why should it concern me in the least when someone I do not like at all thinks badly of me? It is a fact that should make me outrageously happy, or at the very least, indifferent. Then how comes it to overset me?"

Trevina listened to this disjointed tirade and nodded sympathetically. "You have worked too hard of late and are blue-deviled. It happens to all of us at one time or another. What you need is to buy some new gowns, go to a few parties, and flirt shamelessly. Men are the cure to a great many problems," she confided.

"They are also the cause of them," Caroline rejoined with spirit.

"Indeed they are," Trevina admitted readily, "but a flirtation with another man often makes one forget the offending party. I apprehend," she probed carefully, "you formed a tendre for Lord Devlon that he did not reciprocate."

"It is a vast understatement to say that he did not

harbor any kind feelings for me. The man loathed me. But," she continued with a lift of her head, "I did *not* have a tendre for him. I may as well be honest with you," she blurted. "I left Hollowsby because he accused me of stealing."

"He what!" Trevina rose half out of her chair, her mouth open in an expression of disbelief and amazement.

"Accused me of stealing," she repeated sullenly.

"He didn't!" Trevina denied, shocked.

"Oh, but I assure you he did. He thought I'd taken quite a number of family heirlooms."

"How dare he make such improper accusations?"

"Very easily, apparently. And when the missing treasures were found in my room, he felt justified in thinking himself quite correct."

"The man is the veriest coxcomb to have suspected you of such actions. You, of all people! Why, you wouldn't take anything that wasn't yours. Lord Devlon has obviously been misrepresented to me," she declared in indignation. "He can be no better than an ill-bred scoundrel."

Caroline nodded complacent agreement. "Yes. So you see it would have been quite impossible to have formed an attachment to him."

"I should think so! If dear Charles were alive, he should have called the earl out for such words. To speak to you in that manner is reprehensible. Doesn't he know you are a lady?" Trevina demanded, unconsciously pointing the sharp tip of her knife at her companion.

Caroline gently pushed it aside. "That was a subject that appeared to be somewhat in debate in the earl's mind as well."

Trevina set the knife down with a clatter. "Do you mean he not only called you a thief, but he also suggested you might not be a proper person? He inferred you were wanton?" she asked incredulously.

"Well, not precisely," Caroline corrected fairly. "But he said some most unhandsome things to me."

"I should like to tell the cad a few things to his head," Trevina fumed angrily. "You did entirely right to bring Melissa here."

"Yes." Suddenly Caroline did not wish to speak of the earl further. She felt the tears edging into her eyes again, and she didn't want to cry in front of Trevina. Her friend would not have understood the cause of them. She was not sure she did herself.

CHAPTER 15

Lord Devlon walked into the music room and surveyed it critically. The rickety chairs upholstered in dark green cloth bordered in the Greek Key pattern were frayed and discolored as were the draperies of the same design that hung from the long windows. It was obvious a great deal of work was needed in this room as well. He had not been able to fully concentrate on making a list of the repairs needed on the house when it had been filled with women. Now, however, he was free to attend to such details.

The earl's eyes fell on the pianoforte as he walked to the center of the room and looked about. The vision of Caroline playing there flitted through his mind. God, but the chit had been terrible, he recalled with a rueful grin. His smile immediately reversed itself into a frown as Lord Devlon remembered whom he was thinking about. After all, Miss Norton was a woman who had shamelessly stolen from him. In view of that fact, it was surprising the number of times he had thought of Caroline Norton with warmth over the past few days. Sometimes, before the bitterness of what she had done overtook him, he found himself smiling pensively.

"Don't you have a servant in the damned house, Devlon?" a man's cranky voice demanded.

The earl turned in surprise. "Roxby, I was not expecting you."

"Course you weren't," the older man retorted, laying his tall-crowned hat and ebony-tipped cane on a chair as he strode into the room and looked about. "I didn't tell you I was coming. Where are the chits?"

"They have gone," Lord Devlon said tersely.

"I don't wonder why," Roxby snorted as he shrugged out of his greatcoat. "No one could be expected to stay in this tumbledown sty."

"I have servants and workmen due to arrive any day. They will shortly have the house in a much more respectable state. One that I trust will meet with your approval."

"Hope so," Roxby remarked blandly as he settled into the pianoforte chair and picked up a sheet of music. He glanced at it absently.

"Are you come to visit, Roxby?" the earl asked politely.

"I don't know." He opened the lid of the pianoforte and began to tentatively pluck a tune.

Lord Devlon gritted his teeth when he recognized the same piece Caroline had played not a week ago. "When do you expect to know how long you are staying?" he asked, an inflection of impatience creeping into his voice.

"Well, truth to tell," Roxby confided as he continued to play, "that depends on how my talk with you goes today."

"It will continue to go badly if you do not close the lid of that instrument before I slam it shut on your hand," the earl snapped with unhostly frankness.

"Beg pardon," Roxby said unrepentantly. "I didn't know you were so adverse to music. It has charms to soothe savage breasts, you know."

"So I have been informed," the earl said acidly. "Now, if we could kindly change the subject from a discussion of music to what brings you here, I would be most grateful."

"Course," Roxby replied affably. He closed the pianoforte lid and regarded his companion with a stern countenance. "I'll make short work of my business. I've come to talk of Chester's Melissa. I think you should marry her."

Lord Devlon stared at his guest for a startled instant. Then he crossed to a hand bell, picked it up and gave a loud ring. "I'll have some refreshments brought for you while you compose yourself and regain your senses."

"Could use a drink," Roxby agreed pleasantly.

When Frederick eventually arrived, rolling into the room mumbling something that sounded like "curst bells," Lord Devlon directed him to bring a bottle of brandy and two glasses. "Now then." He turned back to his guest. "Why don't you come over here and sit in one of these very uncomfortable-looking chairs, and we can discuss whatever it is you wish."

Roxby glanced at the green chairs indicated. "No

thank you, I shall remain here. It may not be comfortable, but I think it will support my weight. I suggest you have those chairs destroyed, by the by, along with the rest of the furniture. Have some new things sent from London," he advised.

"I shall consider your suggestion," the earl replied as he walked to the mantel and leaned against it. "But I trust you did not travel from Mannly Wood to tell me how to decorate my house."

"Certainly not. I've already told you why I came. It's your duty to marry Miss Courtney," Roxby repeated with conviction.

"I scarcely see how even you arrived at such a bird-witted decision as that," Lord Devlon declared in quelling accents. "In the first place the child is young enough to be my daughter."

"No!" Roxby made a rapid calculation. "Why, you were just entering your salad days when she was born. Were you that precocious, Rye? I knew you could always turn a pretty phrase with the ladies, and I'm persuaded you've warmed the bed of many a pretty damsel, on both sides of the wedding ring—theirs, not yours—but I didn't think even you were sowing your wild oats that young. Weren't you at Eton at the time?"

"That was a manner of speaking," Lord Devlon grated. He turned his attention to pouring a drink for himself and his companion after Frederick returned bearing a tray with glasses and a bottle. "What I mean is that she is too young for me. And even if she were not, she is not my idea of an intellectual companion."

Roxby grunted dismissively. "You want companionship then go to the cock fights or the races with some sporting young bucks. But a wife only need be attractive and biddable. I think she meets both those requirements." Roxby accepted the glass offered to him, stopped for a sip, and continued benevolently, "Like to come to the wedding but I can't. The chit would remember me from her other wedd—. Er, regret I can't be there, but you have my felicitations."

"You may save them. I am not marrying her," Lord Devlon pronounced unequivocally.

"What? Why that's dashed dishonorable! For one thing your brother ruined the child. And for another," Roxby noted with a superior smile, "you're not getting any younger, and it is high time you married and had a parcel of brats to dandle on your knee and spit up on you."

"You make domestic life sound very appealing," Lord Devlon noted dryly. "However, I would have you remember that I am not in my dotage yet. And I fancy when and if I marry it will not be for the reasons you mentioned. I'm not addlepated enough to think I'll be madly in love with any woman I leg-shackle myself to, but I do believe there should be some mutual respect."

"I'm sure the girl respects you." Roxby dismissed that argument with a careless wave of the hand. "What you don't seem to understand is that your brother has soiled the child's reputation. It's your duty as his heir to make up for any misdeeds on his part."

"Were I to attempt to repair all his misdeeds, I rather believe I would find myself married to over a hundred women. You may check the law if you wish, but I believe that is illegal. Besides, my brother did not ruin the child single-handedly," Lord Devlon pointed out with a penetrating look at his guest. "He was aided in his scheme by a certain man who now has the effrontery to suggest I wed a girl not old enough to be out of the schoolroom."

"Then you won't marry the chit?" Roxby pressed.

"I will not," the earl answered firmly.

"All right," Roxby conceded handsomely, "if you won't marry her, I will. As you noted, I did have a hand in her downfall, and I don't have your dashed delusions of having bedroom discussions with a wife concerning Whig politics and the German opera."

Lord Devlon perused Roxby's face with a suspicious look, finished his drink, and poured himself another one before pronouncing with an emphatic nod of his head. "You are mad."

"I'm as sane as ever I was! I see no reason why my marrying the girl is not the perfect solution. I am possessed of some little fortune and I have very few bad habits. I do gamble a bit and take a nip or two now and then. I don't like boiled eggs either, but other than that my domestic life is simple and I think any woman would be pleased to have me."

"Roxby," the earl said ungraciously, "you're even older than Chester was. I don't doubt you're old enough to be the chit's grandfather."

Roxby looked suitably affronted. "Well, I don't *look* my age."

Lord Devlon regarded the portly, balding man in front of him with a suppressed laugh. He looked every bit of his fifty odd years. But whether Roxby looked eighteen or eighty was beside the point. It didn't change the fact that his scheme was preposterous. "This girl is just turned sixteen. My God, Roxby, you have corns that are that old. Take my advice and forget this entire venture. Nothing good can come of it. She really is too young for either of us," Lord Devlon ended on a conciliatory note.

"Well, then, I'm willing to offer for the other one."

"What other one?"

"Her aunt, of course."

"That's totally impossible." Lord Devlon's jaw set in a rigid line and he put his glass down so hard he chipped a piece off the bottom of the crystal goblet.

"Why?" Roxby pressed.

"Miss Norton would not be a suitable wife."

"Well, why not? *She's* old enough, ain't she? And she's not too hard on the eyes, I've heard. And if I married her, the other one could come to live with us. Everything would be taken care of all right and tight and no dishonor to anyone," he concluded with simple satisfaction.

Lord Devlon looked down at the fire and kicked at the smoldering embers before turning back to his guest. "Miss Norton would not be suitable," he repeated in a tight voice.

"Well, damn it, Devlon, what do you suggest? You don't like anything I bring forward, but what are you doing to save both of those women from ending their days as Covent Garden wares?"

The earl said stiffly, "I don't wish to discuss everything I know about Miss Norton. Suffice it to say, she acted less than honestly while she was in my home. I requested her to leave. Under those circumstances I don't believe I owe her anything."

"Maybe not," Roxby said fairly, "but did you turn Miss Courtney out with her?"

The earl looked back at the fire. "She left with her aunt, yes."

"You ought to be ashamed of yourself!" Roxby pronounced, shaking an accusing finger at his host.

Lord Devlon's immediate reaction to defend himself was overruled almost instantly by the knowledge that there was a good deal of truth in Roxby's words. A good deal! They were *entirely* true. Whatever Caroline had done had not been Melissa's fault. And the fact remained, just as Roxby had said, that Melissa had been misused by his brother. It was his duty to make up to her for any pain she may have suffered.

"You can see I'm right, can't you?" Roxby pressed remorselessly.

"Yes." Lord Devlon paced across the room and thrust back a curtain to look out the window. He had not acted as a gentleman. Whatever Miss Norton had done—he clenched his teeth at the thought of her actions—her niece was blameless. The child had lived at Hollowsby, thinking herself the mistress of it. Until the day she had left, it was apparent she had not known she had been Chester's mistress, period. Chester's conduct toward the child had been unforgivable. And his own had been no better, he chastised himself. He had turned Melissa out of the house without the first farthing. Hell, the chit should have every bit of his brother's money and Hollowsby into the bargain.

The fury of the moment when he had discovered his family heirlooms in Miss Norton's room came back to him in all its vividness. He had been so angry at the realization of what she had done that he had given no further thought to Melissa. But now, he knew, he must find her and alleviate any distress she was suffering.

"Well, what are you going to do?" Roxby demanded impatiently.

The earl exhaled his breath slowly. "I shall find Miss Courtney and offer to make whatever amends are necessary. That will include a house and a handsome allowance, as well as endeavoring to ascertain that rumors she was never wed to Chester are not bruited abroad."

"Well, what are you waiting for?" the older man prompted. "You might as well go immediately."

"I don't even know where she is. I will have to make inquiries."

"I can help you there," Roxby offered largely. "Her mother lives in Ireland with a baron. Learned that the other day from a certain young woman who had once spent some time in the company of the baron herself, if you take my meaning." He winked broadly.

"I know what you mean," Lord Devlon replied in clipped tones.

Roxby laughed. "Thought you would. Prime armful that one," he recalled with a reminiscent smile. "Must make a note to see her again."

"Not five minutes ago you were offering to marry this child who has already been deceived by one man," the earl reminded him severely.

"I would have reformed," Roxby defended himself. "However, as I was saying, the mother ain't married, but she's been with this baron a time. She'll doubtless still be there when you get to Ireland. I've written down her direction." He stopped to search through the pockets of the coat lying beside him on the pianoforte and finally extracted a wrinkled piece of paper. "Ah, here it is. Well, now that this is all taken care of, we can enjoy ourselves. I haven't eaten in some time. I trust you will be able to provide me with some food."

"I can," Lord Devlon replied gravely.

"Excellent. I might even stay a few days."

"Not after you taste the food, you won't," the earl predicted. "And if you do you will be alone as I will leave tomorrow for Ireland."

CHAPTER 16

"Lord Devlon! How very kind of you to call," Georgiana greeted her guest effusively.

The earl watched the tall woman who came across the large foyer to greet him. She had curls of brassy yellow piled atop her head and, despite some rather clever artifices with rouge and other aids, she was well past the first blush of youth. Lord Devlon had never met her before, but she looked familiar enough. Her hazel eyes were the same as those of her sister and her features matched Melissa's, only this woman's nose was a little more pronounced than her daughter's retroussé one.

He bowed formally and maintained a dispassionate expression as she extended a ringed hand to him. In truth, he felt a little foolish. Surely she must know of the way he had treated her daughter. In view of those circumstances, he had not expected such a generous welcome.

But the woman before him, dressed in a somber black gown, which fitted tightly and revealed the shape of nature's generosity, beamed a brilliant smile at him.

"Let us not stand in the hall, my lord," she said with a wide sweep of her hand toward a door that stood open at one end of the foyer. "Come into the parlor and I shall have tea sent."

"I really don't wish to impose on you, madame."

"Call me Georgiana," she urged with an easy laugh. "Everyone does." She turned and led him to a large red room and waved him to a camel-back sofa. "I hope you had a good crossing."

"Indeed, I did," he replied, speaking slowly as he looked about the room. He was startled to note the furniture was shrouded in the deep black of mourning. For whom?

"Excellent. You must tell me all about yourself. Melissa is so very shy about discussing you, or anything about England. I daresay it reminds her of her dear departed husband, Hector," she sighed.

"Chester," Lord Devlon corrected politely.

Georgiana continued, unhearing: "The poor child. They were so happily married." She pulled a black-edged handkerchief from the straight sleeve of her gown and dabbed prettily at each eye.

The earl accepted her statement with an outward show of equanimity.

"No doubt, you have come to see your dear sister," she continued. "I shall ring for her."

"Not just yet, if you please," Lord Devlon stopped her from pulling the bell rope. "I wish to speak with you first, if I may."

She seated herself in a chair across from the earl and directed long-lashed eyes at him questioningly.

"I should, of course, have sent a note, but I only

want a few minutes of your time, so I didn't wish to alarm you with a message."

"Alarm us! My dear sir," Georgiana laughed girlishly, "I assure you a visit from anyone as handsome as you are can scarcely be called alarming. Any woman would account herself fortunate indeed to spend time with such a nonpareil as yourself." She picked up an ivory fan from the table beside her and pointed it at him playfully. "I hope my sister was sensible of her good fortune to be able to do so."

Lord Devlon flushed and turned his attention to the floor, carefully examining the deep rose flowers of the Aubusson rug. "Miss Norton and I did not have a chance to become thoroughly acquainted," he said carefully.

"Pity. You would have liked her. She is something of a bluestocking and she doesn't go about in society like she ought, or even *know* many people in the *ton*, but I assure you she is as capable of enjoying herself as any other woman. In the proper way, of course," Georgiana amended loftily.

"Yes. Of course," he mumbled. He was saved from making any further comments by the timely arrival of tea.

As Georgiana poured the tea with theatrical little gestures, she pursued a pleasant monologue, unwittingly giving Lord Devlon time to sort out his thoughts. He had come to Ireland to offer compensation to Melissa for the decidedly shabby way he had treated her. But it was plain her mother had no knowledge of the affair her daughter had been embroiled in or the thievery of which her sister was guilty. That more than a little puzzled him and left him uncertain what course of action to pursue next.

Georgiana's question brought Lord Devlon out of his thoughts. "You will be able to spend some time here, won't you, my lord? In fact," she added as an inducement to that end, "my sister will be arriving next week. She is bringing Melissa's dear little dog with her. My daughter can hardly contain her excitement. I did not know she and Caroline were such good friends; the child is awaiting her arrival with great eagerness."

"I see." he commented mildly. He suspected he knew very well whose arrival Melissa was anticipating. At the thought of Caroline traveling all the way from England with Clover, an animal she despised so heartily, a grin escaped him.

"You're smiling! Does that mean you'll stay to see her?"

He drew himself up straight. He had no intention of staying in Ireland any longer than was necessary to speak with Melissa. And if her aunt was due to arrive shortly, he was doubly certain he would not remain. "I fear I cannot. I have pressing business concerns to attend to. I shall be leaving today after I speak with your daughter."

"Today!" she cried. "What have I said to offend you? You have not come all this distance merely to give your compliments to your sister and then turn around and leave!"

"I did not travel here to pay my respects to your daughter." Now was as good a time as any to disabuse this woman of the idea he was on anything akin to friendship with any member of her family. He had come as a gentleman to correct a very severe error in his treatment of a young lady, and when that task was performed, he intended to leave posthaste.

"I fear I must make my mission clear, madame. I have come to discuss certain financial matters concerning your daughter."

"Surely that is an affair your solicitor can handle," Georgiana dismissed the subject in favor of one of more interest to her. "I must own, I was surprised that Melissa returned to live with me. Although," she hastened to add, "of course she is *quite* welcome and, as you can see," she motioned around the room proudly with an airy gesture, "we are in deep mourning over Lester's death. But," she returned to what was uppermost in her mind, "I had thought dear Melissa could continue on at Hollowsby. You could endeavor to see that a suitably correct woman is engaged to live with her," she suggested baldly.

"Hollowsby is not in a condition for a young girl to be managing," he replied. "It wants extensive work. However, she is welcome to reside at another estate. And I shall, of course, see that a proper chaperon is found for her."

Georgiana's face creased into a contented smile and her shiny golden ringlets bobbed as she nodded happily. "Splendid! I knew you would take everything in hand, my lord. You have the air about you of one who is able to attend to matters directly. That is the way my sister is. You and she really would deal very well together, you know," she said with a sly look from beneath long, curling lashes.

"Yes," he responded gruffly. "I'm sure we should." He changed the subject abruptly. "Could I speak with your daughter now, madame? If you do not wish her to meet me alone I shall understand, but I did have something of a particular nature to discuss."

Georgiana cut him off with a light laugh. "Don't be absurd! Of course you may speak with her alone. You are her brother."

Lord Devlon swallowed that statement silently and waited while she rang the bell and directed the maid who responded to call Melissa. "Tell her I have a marvelous surprise in store for her," Georgiana instructed the maid with a merry smile.

"Now then," she turned back to her guest, still smiling, "I would like to show you some pictures I have just had hung. One of them is of Melissa. She may wish to take it back to England with her." As she spoke, she rose and walked to a row of portraits at one end of the long room. Lord Devlon followed her.

He murmured an appropriate response to the picture of Melissa as a baby, but it was the second portrait that captured his attention. A young Georgiana, dressed in an azure velvet riding habit, sat astride a white horse. Her long blond hair flowed back behind her, and she was smiling a beguiling smile. But it was the girl beside the horse, quietly holding the reins, who held his gaze. A youthful Caroline looked out at him. Her red-gold hair was long and curling and her peacock-blue riding habit was demure and becoming on her girlishly slim figure. Her hazel eyes were soft and thoughtful and her lips were parted in an expression of wistful expectation.

Lord Devlon resisted an urge to reach out his hand and touch the slightly parted lips, to try to coach them into a smile. There was something fragile and unprotected about the girl in the painting and he felt a sudden fierce desire to remedy that.

". . . don't you agree, my lord?" Georgiana asked, her voice raised a little; it seemed not to be the first time she had put the question.

Lord Devlon turned to his hostess. "I beg your pardon. I fear I wasn't attending."

Melissa's arrival prevented Georgiana from replying, but her eyes searched the earl's face with a quizzical look.

Melissa rushed into the room with her cheeks flushed and her voice expectant. She didn't even notice the visitor in her excitement. "Mama, is it true? Is Clover really here?"

"No, my dear. He doesn't come until next week."

"Oh." Her face fell. "I thought you had a surprise."

"And so I have," Georgiana said with a regal inclination of her brass curls toward the earl. "Look who has come to visit you, my dear."

Melissa's face fell even further as she beheld Lord Devlon moving toward her. She stood stunned while he took her limp hand.

"I trust I find you in good health?" Lord Devlon asked pleasantly.

"Oh," she said faintly. "Oh, dear."

"Really," her mother admonished, "that is no way to receive such a distinguished guest. He is your brother." She turned to the earl with a nervous laugh. "Her grief, you understand, quite oversets her at times, and she doesn't know what she is doing." She directed her words to Melissa. "Lord Devlon has come a considerable distance to speak with you. He has something he most particularly wishes to say in private."

"Oh," she repeated, her face growing pale. "In private?"

"Yes," Lord Devlon replied quietly, "your mother has graciously consented."

"Dear me, indeed yes! Take all the time you need," Georgiana exhorted and left with a merry wave of her handkerchief. Melissa watched her go with the expression of one who has just received word they are to be beheaded.

"Won't you be seated?" the earl asked solicitously after the door closed behind Georgiana.

Melissa appeared not to have heard him. Instead she paced the room in obvious agitation, looking at him from time to time with fearful glances.

"I have come to talk of money," he began. He was still standing politely, waiting for her to seat herself. When she did not, he continued: "There is not the least need to be afraid of me. I know I behaved quite inappropriately the day you left. In fact, my conduct until that point had not been altogether above reproach. But I wish to make amends for any injustice that has been done to you by my family."

She stopped in her perambulation and gazed at him in surprise.

"I am prepared to make a very handsome settlement on you. I shall, of course, provide you with a suitable estate on which to live and will also engage a companion for you. I think in a year or two you could be introduced into society, although you could not have a come-out, since you have been married. I shall do my utmost to assure your position among the *ton*. I will also ascertain that no gossip concerning the unfortunate events of your wedding ever gets abroad. You will be a widow in the eyes of everyone."

Melissa continued to stare at him with her eyes round and her mouth pursed in an expression of amazement.

"Is that not enough? If there is something further you wish, you have only to say so. Since even your mother is unaware of the circumstances of your marr—er, your association with my brother, I do not think it would be a difficult matter to stanch any rumors. Your aunt, I am persuaded, would never divulge your secret."

"You mean to give me money and a house?" Melissa asked dazedly.

"Yes." The earl's patience was wearing rather thin.

"Why?" she asked simply.

"Because it is the gentlemanly thing to do." Why did she think? he wondered uncomfortably.

"Then you do not know about the treasures that were stolen?"

"Of course I do," he said irritably. "But just because your aunt has behaved improperly, *you* should not be punished."

Melissa sank onto the black-draped sofa and regarded him in despair. "My aunt did not behave improperly," she whispered.

Lord Devlon suppressed a sigh of exasperation. He had no desire to argue such an obvious point. Neither did he wish to talk of Miss Norton any more than was absolutely necessary. He got the most afflicting pains in the hollow of his stomach when he did.

"I took the treasures, my lord."

It was the earl's turn to look surprised. He regarded her in silence for a moment and then asked with exquisite politeness, "I beg your pardon?"

Melissa began slowly and then continued faster, as if the floodgates had been opened and she was powerless to hold back the flow. "When you arrived at Hollowsby you seemed so angry. And you were intent that we should leave, everyone, even Clover. I didn't wish to stay and argue with you because you seemed very dark and fearsome, only Auntie Caro said she would not let you flummery us. She said we must stay and keep possession of the house. But I knew you would turn us out, and I wanted to go. Only I had no money to leave and I wasn't certain Mama would want me to come here to live and I thought— Well, they were such small things really, just little vases and the like. Who would have missed them? And the bust, I'm sorry I broke it, but it was my favorite and the hall was full of them, so I didn't think it would signify if I took it as a keepsake." She ended on a forlorn note and looked at the rug in absolute dejection.

There was silence for several moments before Lord Devlon asked, "Your aunt knew nothing of this?"

Melissa shook her head mournfully. "I only put the things in her room the morning you discovered them. And then I was too frightened to confess when Auntie Caro said you were so wildly angry."

There was another silence before Lord Devlon cleared his throat and said calmly. "I see. Of course this changes nothing in the offer I have made today. I shall send my solicitor to make final arrangements. I shall also send Miss Norton a note of apology." As if he were speaking to himself, he added, "I daresay, since your aunt is a companion, it made it somehow all seem very plausible that she would need money and therefore was the likely person to have taken the heirlooms. I see I have wronged her."

Melissa looked at him in confusion. "My aunt is not a companion."

"I understood she lived in Wiltshire with a widow who had two small children."

"Yes, she went there at her friend's invitation, but she is not employed in that capacity; she only does it as a favor."

"Yes, I see." He ran a restless hand through his hair. "I shall send her a note, as I have said. I have wronged her greatly and would like to make amends."

CHAPTER 17

Caroline straightened in the chair in her sunny sitting room and reread the letter she held before her.

"My dear Miss Norton," it began in a large masculine scrawl, "Since your departure from Hollowsby, I have learned how gravely erroneous my accusations against you were. I beg your forgiveness most humbly. There is much I wish to say to you. In short, I feel I owe you a good deal more than a mere apology. I beg your permission to call upon you at your convenience. Your obedient servant, Lord Devlon."

She folded the letter carefully and then immediately unfolded it and read it yet again. The earl had undoubtably found the servant guilty of the thefts. And now he wished her forgiveness! She tilted her head haughtily. And well he should beg!

The agreeable thought of the earl squirming uncomfortably under her implacable gaze held a moment's appeal for Caroline. She considered it with the self-righteous indignation of one whose revenge seems near at hand. In fact, the vision conjured up was so enjoyable, Caroline gazed out the window of her silver and green room for some minutes with a half-smile playing on her lips before she roused herself to read the missive once again.

This time she detected an undercurrent in the note which had escaped her before. Wasn't there something more conveyed in the letter than a desire to ask her forgiveness? What did "I owe you a good deal more than a mere apology" mean? Surely he didn't think to offer her money? That would be totally indecorous.

Caroline crumpled the letter in her hand with a sudden fierce movement. Lord Devlon had thoroughly humiliated her. Well, she would not give him the opportunity to ease his guilty conscience. He did not deserve that she should grant him an interview, she thought waspishly. He had treated her as an object of scorn and she would repay in kind.

Mobilized into action, Caroline rose from her chair and crossed the room to the drop leaf cherry desk. She took a fine piece of parchment from a neat stack, stabbed the pen into the standish, and scribbled furiously. "Lord Devlon, I have received your message, but I find myself unable to comply with your request for a visit. Yours, Miss Norton."

Caroline read the note aloud and sighed. No, it wouldn't serve. She must write the earl a dignified letter accepting his apology but declining to receive him. Whatever his actions toward her had been, she must remain a lady, even though it meant denying herself a great deal of satisfaction and some little justice.

Reluctantly she drew another sheet of paper off the stack and began more slowly. "My Lord Devlon,

I accept your gracious apologies concerning certain misunderstandings that occurred during my recent stay in Dorset. It is, however, totally unnecessary for you to call, and I wouldn't wish for you to go to so much trouble. I thank you for your kind letter. I remain your humble servant, Miss Caroline Norton."

She sanded the letter lightly and folded it carefully. Then she drew out another sheet and began a letter to Georgiana. After all, she needed to apprise her sister that she would not be coming to visit but was sending Clover to the island in the company of a rather disgruntled groom. And there was also the desire to unburden herself of her feeling toward the earl.

"Dear Georgiana," she scribbled, "I shall not be able to come to visit you, but Melissa's dog will arrive as soon as he may be persuaded to board the coach. I hope Melissa goes on well without him. All is well here. I am glad to be back with Trevina and away from the odious earl. I am certain Melissa has told you how we suffered at his hands. I hope that I shall not be forced to deal with him ever again, or I shall not be responsible for my actions as he really is too, too tiresome to bear. But then, I am certain you have met men like that—men who can be charming and flattering when it suits them but who are, underneath, unscrupulous creatures. I shall write more details when there is news of Clover's decision on boarding the carriage."

She signed her name and then added a hasty postscript, "Tell Melissa I have received a letter from

Lord Devlon. He asked permission to see me, but I declined."

Caroline sealed both letters and proceeded slowly to the breakfast room. Even in her state of self-righteous indignation against the earl she was not so dishonest with herself as to deny that she did want to see him. She could not, of course, because she would certainly disgrace herself utterly by ending up in tears at the sight of him. Caroline couldn't bear the thought of demeaning herself so in his presence. At least he could leave her her pride; she would save her tears for the privacy of her bedroom, where they seemed to be a more and more frequent visitor.

The problem was, she admitted grudgingly, that she cared for Lord Devlon. There was no reason why she should. No earthly reason. But she did. Unbidden thoughts of him haunted her in her waking and sleeping hours. She saw him with his dark hair wind-tossed and his eyes laughing. Caroline straightened in her chair. Any feelings she had for the earl would eventually pass. She had only to direct her attention elsewhere and soon he would be nothing more than a faint memory. The ridiculous desire she felt to be in his arms would be completely stifled.

"Auntie Caro," Katie's small voice broke into her thoughts as she sat at the breakfast table. "Mama said to ask you if we might put a small saddle on the doggie and ride him about the yard. She didn't think we ought, but I'm sure he wants to play. And we wouldn't pull his tail, although Julia did pull Pussy's last week. But she got a fearsome scratch, and I don't think she would pull Doggie's. Can we ride him? Please!"

"Certainly not," Caroline replied firmly and put Lord Devlon from her mind to deal with day-to-day life in Trevina's household.

The earl received the letter from Frederick with an impatience he was hard-pressed to conceal. The swirling script on the envelope told him clearly it was in a feminine hand; he strongly suspected it was his reply from Miss Norton. He broke the seal and extracted the letter, still standing in the rotunda in his riding clothes.

After reading it through rapidly, he muttered a succinct curse and then read it more carefully, an action that put him even more out of temper. Caroline had refused to see him but in a very refined manner. She had not availed herself of the opportunity to cut him dead. She had accepted his apologies cordially and made a polite but firm refusal to receive him.

He tossed his riding crop and beaver hat onto a table and stamped up to his room. Her rejection, nicely phrased but a rejection nonetheless, should have put an end to the matter. But it did not. Instead Lord Devlon found himself even more determined to see Miss Norton.

"Damn her," he repeated aloud as his valet helped him out of his well-cut brown waistcoat. He had a right to tender his regrets personally. After that he would leave her and never disturb her further. He wanted only to be allowed to be a gentleman.

No, he admitted wearily, that was not the truth. His reasons for wanting to see Miss Norton were more complex than the mere desire to redeem himself in her eyes and to establish that he was a gentleman. He could not explain, even to himself, exactly what his feelings for her were, but he knew he wanted her to respect him and like him.

He had behaved with shocking rudeness to her. Oh, it had all seemed perfectly justified at the time. He had thought her a fortune seeker and adventuress and had called her as much. Now that he was aware of the extent of his misjudgment, he felt guilty and angry with himself. She was probably in the right of it to refuse to see him. Had the circumstances been reversed, he didn't doubt he would have torn the message to bits and sent it back with no reply. She had shown forbearing to write him a considerate, if not warm, note. That missive gave him hope. Perhaps if he wrote again and she saw that he really did wish to see her and was not just trying to observe the amenities, she would consent to allow him to visit her.

That decision made, he returned to his study and searched for some words that could adequately express how remorseful he felt. The note he finally penned did not convey his feelings but it was the best he could manage. Besides, the fact that he had sent a second letter would surely convince Miss Norton that he was sincere in wishing to see her.

But even as he posted the letter, he was uncertain whether she would accept his request to visit her. He had briefly considered riding to Wiltshire and calling on Miss Norton without her permission but had decided against that course. He did not wish to force himself on her; it would only make her think the less of him. Her opinion of him was low enough already.

During the days that he awaited her reply, the earl tried to occupy himself with plans for the house and property. But he often found himself gazing out the window and considering what he would say to Miss Norton should she agree to receive him. He gave little thought to the apology he would make but a great deal to how to pave his way for future calls.

Perhaps after a few months had passed he and Caroline Norton could be friends. He would like to have her friendship. He thought she had not been wholly indifferent to him, although he knew her sensibilities had been severely wounded by his accusations. If he went slowly, he was confident he could reestablish the lighthearted feeling that had existed between them in the week before the discovery of the family heirlooms.

A week after he had posted his letter to Caroline, Lord Devlon was sitting in his study on a sunny afternoon surveying the plans he had just completed for the work on the drawing room. He glanced up as Frederick appeared at the open door with a battered brass dish that contained a note in a now-familiar swirling script. The earl put aside his plans nonchalantly.

"Mail, I see," he said casually.

" 'Tis the letter ye been waitin' fer," Frederick announced cheerfully.

"What?"

Nonplussed, Frederick elaborated, "Ye been waitin' about 'ere for somethin', I'll be bound, or ye would have been in London long since."

"I am seeing to the renovation of my house," Lord Devlon said crisply.

"Sure ye are," the servant agreed placidly, "but your face ain't lighted up like that over any of the ren'vations. Ye looked like a boy bein' given the biggest cookie in the jar, ye did," he chuckled as he stroked his flowing white beard.

"I shall summon you if I need you further," Lord Devlon dismissed his servant. He waited for Frederick to turn and walk to the door, affecting an interest in his plans until the door closed. Then he shoved the blueprints aside and tore the letter open.

"My dear Lord Devlon, I beg you will not distress yourself further over my well-being. I am fine and hope you are also. Again I must decline your generous offer to call upon me. It is quite unnecessary. And I shan't be in Wiltshire any longer, at any rate," she had added as a teasing conclusion, "Yours, Caroline Norton."

Lord Devlon folded the note with dignity, took the plans out, and proceeded to look them over. There was not the least need to give any more thought to Miss Norton, he concluded, as he regarded the blueprints with studious interest, quite unaware he had them upside down.

CHAPTER 18

"This is most tiresome and inconvenient," Caroline muttered. And those were not the worst of her thoughts. She could have said a great deal more about her journey, which would have been even less charitable. From the beginning, when she had received Georgiana's urgent message telling her to join them in Devonshire, Caroline wished she could refuse. Whatever was her sister doing in Devonshire, anyway, Caroline wondered impatiently. She herself didn't know a living soul who resided in that shire, although she didn't doubt it was inhabited. And, even more exasperating, had been Georgiana's scribbled postscript stating it was a matter of the utmost urgency, and the happiness of one of the people dear to Georgiana depended on Caroline's coming.

There was hardly any way to deny such a message. Then, of course, she had been concerned that something might be amiss with Melissa. It was always very difficult to discover with Georgiana where fact left off and her own active imagination took up. Perhaps there was nothing wrong at all.

Caroline peered out the window of the carriage

203

once again. Sighing, she pulled her head back in and tried unsuccessfully to settle back against the squabs and relax. It was an attempt that was considerably hampered by the quality of the driving. The carriage was first on one side of the road and then on the other. The driver, she had long since determined, must be quite drunk. That thought made her uneasy.

She glanced at her maid—a slender young woman in a dull blue cloak who was looking nervously out the window. "Do you think the driver knows what he is about?" the maid asked as she turned her plain face toward her mistress with an anxious expression.

"No, Clara, but there is precious little we can do about it now. We shall simply have to wait until he stops at the next inn to refresh the horses, and I shall speak with him. If he is simply bosky, we shall remain there until a replacement can be found or until he sobers up. Maybe," she added, "he isn't drunk, only a very poor driver."

"Perhaps," the maid agreed unhappily. "I hope he isn't one of these young men who race each other along the roads for bets."

Caroline said nothing, but she doubted that possibility. She fancied she knew Quality when she saw them, and the short, stocky, ill-shaven man who was driving the coach did not have the manners of Quality, although he was one of Trevina's servants whom she had never seen before.

The carriage hit a particularly deep rut and Caroline's head bounced up against the ceiling, squashing her corn-yellow satin bonnet bordered in dark-red velvet and doing considerable damage to her temper as well. She pulled the check string angrily but the vehicle continued on its way. "Doesn't he hear me?" Caroline demanded in irritation.

Clara, looking white and shaken, shook her head hopelessly. "He hasn't answered when you have pulled it before."

Caroline closed her eyes in frustration and tried to keep her head from bouncing about so much. She had been much in sympathy with Clover over the last few miles of the journey. The same nausea he must have experienced was now afflicting her. She swallowed heavily and tried to think of something cheerful to rouse herself from this low state of mind.

Caroline was wrenched out of her thoughts as the carriage swayed crazily to left and right.

"Lord help us!" Clara screeched.

Caroline had only time to grasp again for the check string before the vehicle gave a final wild lunge and fell heavily on its side.

Within the carriage, confusion reigned as boxes and people fell toward what had been the right side of the coach and was now the bottom. Clara fell atop Caroline in a tangle of limbs, and boxes cascaded down on the pair of them while Clara whimpered and Caroline muttered darkly.

It was a moment or two before Clara recovered herself enough to ease off her mistress as far as she was able, which, lamentably, was not far.

Clara murmured apologetically, "So sorry to be on you like this."

"Don't be a goose. You obviously cannot help it.

Let us see if we can stand and pull ourselves out through the window."

As they moved to attempt that feat, they were halted by the sound of an authoritative voice. "Stay put in there! I shall take care of everything."

"If that is the groom, he already has taken care of everything," Caroline said in a voice that boded ill for the man.

The door above them opened and a head appeared. Both women looked at the florid-faced man with bright red hair who smiled down at them. "I'm a doctor, dear ladies. Fear not! I shall take good care of you." He accompanied his words by extending two chubby arms inward toward them. Caroline stood shakily and the doctor helped her climb out. From there he assisted her onto the ground.

"Any bones broken?" he asked heartily.

"You are the doctor," she said crisply.

"Ah, yes, so I am. Damn good one at that too, if I do say so myself. Yes. And what is your name, my dear?" he asked with formal courtesy.

"Please help my maid out," Caroline said. What a perfectly dull-witted question to ask at a time like this.

"Certainly, certainly, my pleasure to assist her. Hippocratic oath and all, you know." The round little man in his white doctor's frock coat continued talking as he assisted Clara from the vehicle and onto the ground. She dusted off her clothes while Caroline looked angrily at the groom, who was working to calm the horses.

"Well, well," the doctor said. "Are you hurt?"

"No," Caroline answered, "but I cannot be responsible for the groom's health."

"He doesn't appear injured." The man beside her flicked a glance toward the groom.

"Just wait," Caroline promised.

"Calm yourself, my dear. Permit me to introduce myself. I'm Dr. Leech."

"Dr. Leech?" Clara said timidly. "What an odd name for a doctor."

"Yes, bit of it. Parents named me that hoping I'd enter the noble medical profession."

"But that's your last name," Caroline said.

"Yes, indeed it is. Most astute of you, my dear. Quick thinking, I should say. I'm surprised you can think at all after the accident you have had. You look all green."

"I am certain you are concerned for my health, sir," Caroline replied, "but I assure you I am well. I need only determine that the groom and horses are also well. Then we shall see about sending to the nearest village to have some men sent to help put the carriage right."

"My poor child," he said sagely, his face losing its smile to reveal large drooping jowls, "I have been in this profession countless long years. I know the signs of sickness. You look quite ill; I don't doubt you have sustained an injury. Since it is growing late, I must insist you allow me to take you to the nearest house. There I can examine you and your maid. She also looks a bit peaked."

Caroline glanced about her. "I don't see a house," she replied, her mind working to sort out why the land looked familiar, while also trying to ascribe a locale to the doctor's peculiar accent. "I really must insist you allow me to go along. I am on urgent business."

"Ma'am, your next business will be your own funeral if you do not permit me to help." His busy red eyebrows lowered on his round face, making him look ominous.

"I don't feel altogether the thing," Clara joined in plaintively.

"Quite right. Now, if you both would be so kind as to step into my carriage, I shall take you to the closest house."

Caroline capitulated. "Very well." She allowed the doctor to hand her into his carriage and she settled herself in with a final malevolent look at the groom before the door closed. Within, all was darkness.

"Very sorry about that," the doctor spoke in the blackness, startling Caroline. "My vehicle is sometimes used to convey bodies. Have to haul the dead as well as the living," he noted jovially. "Needn't worry the least bit. Your maid is here with you so all's right and proper. Yes, indeed. Pity, you can't see the scenery, but there's precious little about anyway."

"Exactly where am I, sir? Our driver was driving so recklessly that I have been quite unable to look out the window and discover where we were any time these last three hours."

"Somewhere in Dorset," he replied vaguely.

"I know that," Caroline said with a tight hold on her waning patience, "but exactly where in Dorset?"

"Southern part," he elaborated briefly. "Now, my dear lady, enough of such trite matters. Do you recall your name? Sometimes severe jolts such as you have suffered result in a loss of memory."

"Of course I know my name," Caroline replied. "I am Miss Caroline Norton. This is my maid." Caroline pointed to the woman seated beside her but quickly returned her hand to her lap as she realized the doctor could not see it.

The two parties mumbled greetings, and polite commonplaces were exchanged by the three until the carriage lurched to a stop.

"Must be there," the doctor murmured and opened the door. He descended and reached a hand up to help Caroline alight. Emerging from the darkness, she blinked to adjust her eyes to the change in light and looked about with a gasp of recognition. "This is Hollowsby!"

"What's that?" he asked loudly, helping the maid out as he spoke and then bustling back to put a guiding hand under Caroline's arm to assist her up the stairs.

"I'm not going in there," she whispered, standing firm and staring at the house as if it were a revolting sight rather than the perfectly stately Georgian house it was. She turned to face Dr. Leech. "I will not go into that house. I know the inhabitant and I have no wish to see him."

"My dear madame," the doctor said sternly. "You are proving a most obstinate patient. I regret that we are not in the vicinity of some particular friend's home, but I do think you must give over this ceaseless arguing. Circumstances have combined to bring you to this house and I say it's placed opportunely. You will not be obliged to stay here one minute longer than is absolutely necessary, but I must insist you allow me to see that all is well before I release you to travel off into the unknown. It is," he concluded with ponderous gravity, "my obligation to humanity to tend to the sick. Even if you are not injured, your maid may well be."

Caroline turned a guilty face to Clara. In her wish to avoid entering the mansion she had not fully considered her maid might need medical attention. "Very well. I shall go within and remain while you make certain Clara is well enough to travel again. After that I wish to leave."

"That is perfectly acceptable to me," he replied stiffly. "I don't do this for my amusement, you know."

Caroline managed a small smile of repentance. "I beg your pardon, sir. You are doing your utmost to care for us and I am making it exceedingly difficult, am I not?" She offered him her arm. "I shall go in and I promise I shan't raise any more objections."

"Excellent," he grunted.

Caroline permitted the doctor to guide her up the steps while Clara followed behind. She must indeed have suffered some ill effects from the accident, she considered, because her knees were shaking and she felt chilly all over. As they reached the top steps, the door was opened by Frederick, who gave the assembled visitors a surprised look but bid them follow him after Doctor Leech gave curt instructions they were to be shown to a bedroom.

"Frederick," Caroline asked weakly as she trudged after him up the stairs, "is—is Lord Devlon at home?"

"No," Frederick said and then was too overcome by his habitual hacking to manage any further words.

"Sounds bad, that," the doctor noted sympathetically. "I shall have a look at you when I am finished with my other patients."

Frederick favored the kind doctor with a withering look and turned to lead them down the hall.

"Might be able to do something about that awkward walk, too," Dr. Leech added further encouragement.

The servant muttered some unintelligible words as he led the threesome into a sitting room that adjoined a bedroom.

"This will do nicely," the doctor acknowledged cheerfully as he looked about the sparsely furnished, drab, brown room. He continued on into the bedroom and directed Caroline to be seated on the bed.

She obeyed and was rewarded with an uncomfortable pain. How embarrassing that the only part of her body to suffer an injury was the rather delicate member she was now seated upon. But she had not the least notion of mentioning that to the doctor! No doubt, it would heal of its own accord.

"Lie down on the bed, Miss Norton."

Caroline did so, gingerly easing up her feet. She

laid stiffly, looking up at the ceiling and affecting nonchalance.

While Clara hovered nearby, the physician removed Caroline's kid slippers and gently felt around on each foot, examining each toe in turn. It was with the greatest of efforts that Caroline was able to steel herself enough to stifle the laughter his tickling touch provoked.

Finally he laid her right foot down and stood. The look on his face chased away Caroline's pent-up laughter. Wiping his hands very carefully on a towel Clara held for him, he said with a look of grave concern, "My dear, I scarcely know how to tell you this—you are so young."

"Tell me what?"

"I fear you have—" He broke off and turned away from her, apparently unable to continue.

"What is wrong with me?" she demanded.

He recovered himself enough to face her, but his bushy eyebrows trembled and his mouth quivered as he shook his head regretfully. "Alas, my child, you have, that most rare and dreaded of all injuries and diseases—the Red Ague."

CHAPTER 19

Caroline lay stiffly on the bed, scarcely daring to move. Why her? Why must she have such a wretched disease, and one with such horrid consequences? Her hair would fall out and her eyes would cross if she did not obey the strict orders Dr. Leech had left. And that was not the worst of the dreaded symptoms of this heartless disease. She would develop a terrible limp and pains would shoot up and down her legs when she tried to walk.

Caroline shifted carefully on the bed and continued to stare upward at the ceiling. She had never even heard of the Red Ague until the doctor had confirmed his diagnosis.

"But how could it have been brought on by a carriage accident?" she had demanded.

He studied her regretfully, wiped a tear from his eye, and told her kindly: "Doubtless, it has been coming on for some time, but it was greatly aggravated by the jolt of the accident."

"But how do you *know* I have it?"

"It's the toes," he told her gloomily. "I can always tell by the way they discolor."

"But I felt no pain when you examined my feet. In fact, it tickled!"

He shook his head remorsefully and took his leave, while Caroline had called after him her earnest assurances that she would do just as he had told her. She would remain in bed for the next two weeks, she would drink the drafts he had ordered for her, and she would be very pleasant to anyone who came to visit. Oversetting herself was the most serious thing she could do, he had warned.

"But Lord Devlon—that is—well, he won't come to see me, will he? Please ask him not to, or I am almost certain I shall overset myself," she had appealed.

"I am only a poor doctor," he replied, "but I shall tell his lordship that it might be for the best for him not to come. If he does visit," he stressed sternly, "you must try to be cheerful and not allow yourself any anxiety over his visit."

She had nodded mutely, her head making swishing noises as it slid back and forth on the satin cover of the pillow. She could only hope the earl, in his surprise at finding her in his house, did not come to her room. It would be embarrassing for both of them, she fretted. If it was fate that she see him, she wished it could be under other circumstances—not while she was flat on her back.

Caroline needn't have worried that Lord Devlon would rush to her room. Indeed, at that very moment he was occupied with concerns of his own. Seated across from him in a Windsor chair in his book-lined study was Georgiana, looking for all the world like a Cheshire cat who had just dined in comfort upon her mistress's canary.

"Thank you for showing my guest in." Lord Devlon turned to Frederick, who still lingered at the door. "I shall call you if I need you."

Frederick made a reluctant departure, obviously curious to know why there was a sudden influx of company.

"Now then," Lord Devlon said as he seated himself, "what can I do to be of assistance to you?"

"I," she informed him grandly, "am doing you a service."

"Then you have my most sincere appreciation," he said politely. When she merely nodded and smiled, he asked, "Might I ask what that service is?"

"Upstairs," Georgiana stopped to point a delicately frilled parasol upwards, "is the object of your affection. I have arranged the whole of it." She carefully smoothed the skirts of her black velvet gown, adjusting the lace at the sleeves with care.

The earl regarded his desk top with gravity and considered how best to rid himself of this woman. She quite obviously did not have her full wits about her. No wonder her daughter was simple: it was plain to see how she had come by it.

"Ah, I see you do not understand what I am speaking about," she gurgled in delight.

"I confess, I do not," he replied courteously. "Perhaps you are overly fatigued from your journey. Let me ring for some tea, unless you would prefer something stronger?" He stopped and raised a questioning brow. It could be the woman was only drunk.

Georgiana lowered her purple parasol with dignity and said smoothly, "My dear sir, I am not in the least interested in refreshments. I am trying to tell you something of importance. My sister, Caroline, is at this very moment in your bedroom upstairs." She settled back in the chair and smiled happily.

"In my bedroom?" he repeated in confusion.

"Not yours," she allowed, "but *one* of yours. She has had a carriage accident and is unable to be moved."

Lord Devlon jumped up and started toward the door. "Good God, woman! Why didn't you tell me? She needs to be seen by a doctor immediately! Is she badly hurt? No, don't answer that; I am afraid I should only be more confused and upset when you finished speaking."

"Do sit down," Georgiana invited with a laugh. "You do not understand, but I shall endeavor to explain it."

He stopped at the door and eyed the calmly smiling woman in the chair. Mad, quite obviously mad. Perhaps Caroline was not upstairs after all. He felt a definite sinking of his spirits. Of course she was not. This woman was a veritable raving maniac.

"My sister," she continued blandly, "was on her way to Devonshire at my request. I sent her an urgent message to meet me there. On the way her carriage overturned, hard by your gates, as a matter of fact, and she was brought here. A doctor has already seen to her, and he has pronounced her unable to move for two weeks."

"What is wrong with her?"

"Nothing."

"I see," Lord Devlon said quietly.

"Don't be ridiculous. How could you see?" she demanded impatiently. "The doctor who confined her to bed is not a physician. He is a baron."

"Of course he is, madame," Lord Devlon agreed, still standing by the door indecisively. "And who am I?" he ventured.

"You are Lord Devlon," she snapped.

At least she didn't think he was Napoleon, he considered.

"My lord," she said firmly, "I am trying to tell you I realize you are in love with my sister, and I am giving you a chance to be together again, an opportunity you made poor work of the last time she was here."

His hand dropped from the door handle and he stared at her in disbelief. "I beg your pardon?" he asked stiffly.

"Don't be cold and distant with me," she reproved, pulling her black gloves up and inspecting them carefully. "That won't serve at all, although I daresay my addlepated sister was taken in by your show of indifference. But *I* can tell when a man is in love. I have had a fair amount of experience in that area," she plumed herself modestly. "From the expression on your face when you saw Caroline's picture, I could see how it is with you."

"Then perhaps you can also deduce how it is with Miss Norton. Even if I were to have a slight spark of interest in her, she abhors me."

"Spark," she sniffed, "a forest fire, more like. You

are madly in love with her and she is—" Georgiana paused and gave him a coy smile. "Let us say I believe she is mildly intrigued with you."

"And what has she said to lead you to that conclusion?" he asked.

"Said? My dear sir, I have not spoken with her since she met you. But my daughter let fall a few things that made me suspect Caroline was acting tolerably peculiar for a woman whose feelings were unattached. And then I received a singularly dull-witted letter from Caroline that confirmed my suspicions."

"And may I ask, madame, what you now intend to do?"

"I? Nothing. I am not a meddler," she informed him virtuously.

"Indeed," he replied faintly.

"I shall be leaving immediately, but Melissa will be arriving shortly."

"You came all the way from Ireland to execute this mad scheme?" he asked in disbelief.

"I needed a new bonnet also," Georgiana confided, "and I had a mind to buy it in London."

"Indeed."

She stretched her hand out to him with a flourish. "I apprehend, you think my wits have gone begging, but you shall see." She gave him a provocative shake of one long, gloved finger. "And you will thank me for this. Caroline is under strict orders to remain in your house for two weeks. I think that will give you ample time to use your charm to woo her."

"Madame," Lord Devlon said, hardly knowing

why he bothered to ask the question, "I find it hard to credit that you were able to arrange for Miss Norton to travel past my house and then concoct a spell to cause her to wreck there." As a worried afterthought he asked, "You are not a believer in witchcraft, are you?"

"Don't be ridiculous. The only spell that induced the groom to overturn the carriage right outside your gates was the magic of seeing a twenty-pound note waved beneath his nose. I must give him something else, as he really did excel in his job."

"Excel! He could have killed her!"

"Fustian! He is far too good for that. Now then," she rose and fluttered her hand toward him. "I simply must be on my way. My baron awaits, no doubt convulsed with laughter and toasting our success. Don't," she cautioned as he held the door open for her and escorted her out into the hall, "make a mull of your courting after all my hard work, my lord. I shan't," she threatened severely, "assist you again."

"I should not dream of asking you to," Lord Devlon murmured as Frederick held the front door open and she breezed out, throwing an airy kiss backward as she went. "I shall not stray far from here. I am anxious for reports."

Frederick closed the door with a grunt. "Just when I thought we 'ad the 'ouse cleared, it's filled back up again. And this time with a sick one."

The earl gave Frederick a slow grin before turning to walk back toward the study. So Caroline was in the house, lying upstairs even now. He paused and looked toward the ceiling. He wondered what sort of temper that young lady was in. Not good, he'd wager. Well, he'd give her a few hours to regain her dignity, then he would pay a polite call.

He stepped back into the study and poured himself a glass of brandy from a crystal decanter on a side table. Savoring the mellow liquid slowly, he chuckled aloud.

So fate, or Georgiana, had seen fit to throw him and Miss Norton together again? Very well, he would make the most of his opportunity. It was ironic that when he had first arrived at Hollowsby and found Miss Norton in residence he could think of nothing he wished more than to rid the house of her and her niece. Now he was inordinately pleased that she was back.

But circumstances had changed, he reflected. When he had first met her, he had had no idea how deep his attachment for her would become. He could not say precisely when his reserve had melted and he had begun to harbor a warm regard for her. It might have been the day they went for a drive about the estate and stopped beside the ocean. He had been much struck by how carefree and happy she had been. Perhaps his feelings had begun to deepen even before that. At any rate, Caroline was in his house now and he meant to use the time while she was under his roof to become her friend once again. After that, he would go very cautiously. He didn't wish to frighten her.

The servants and workmen had arrived only four days before, but they had already wrought some changes in the neglected old house. The rooms were clean, if not newly decorated; and the food, under the new cook, was delicious. Yes, he thought with a nod of contentment, Miss Norton would be most comfortable here.

Satisfied with that thought, he conferred with the new estate manager for some hours, and it wasn't until nearly six that evening that he started up the steps to Miss Norton's room. He fancied she had had ample time to rest and accustom herself to the idea that she would have to remain here for two sennights. He looked forward to seeing her. He might even stay and dine with her.

Lord Devlon stopped outside Caroline's room and tapped gently at the door.

It was opened by a tall, dark woman in a plain navy serge gown.

"I am Lord Devlon. If your mistress is awake, I should like to speak with her to ascertain if she is well."

"Of course, my lord. Please wait and I shall tell her you are here." She rushed off to perform that mission and returned a moment later to lead him into the bedroom.

He walked slowly toward the bed. "Ah, Miss Norton, I trust you are feeling better."

Caroline turned her head fractionally from her rigid position and looked at Lord Devlon out of the corner of her eye as he seated himself on a straight-backed chair next to the bed. "You will forgive me for not rising," she said with a weak smile.

The earl laughed good-naturedly. "Under the circumstances I should not expect it. How do you feel?"

"I have had more enjoyable moments in my life. But, I daresay, I shouldn't complain. I suppose I am lucky to be alive."

"Yes, er, well," Lord Devlon changed the subject from the question of her health. "We have a new cook now and I think you will find the food much improved."

But Caroline, with the lamentable habit of all invalids, wished to discuss only her illness. "The doctor ordered me to move as little as possible and he said I was to be in bed for two weeks. Surely I won't be obliged to lie on my back the whole of that time?"

"I really cannot say," the earl replied evasively.

"I don't think the physician who examined me was from around here," she continued, as if thinking aloud. "Perhaps you would be good enough to ask the village apothecary to send something for me."

"Certainly," he replied. Watching Caroline lying board flat, evidently afraid to move, he felt a pang of guilt. "Miss Norton, I should like to say I am deeply conscious of the wrong I did you when last you were at Hollowsby. I shall do my best possible to make up for my unfortunate actions."

Her eyes slid away from his. "You needn't speak of it."

"But I must. I am sensible that you did not wish to see me. You had, in fact, refused my requests to call upon you. You must now feel most uncomfortable to be in my house. I beg, you will not consider my past actions but will permit me to make amends to you in whatever ways I can."

"Of course," she murmured. She looked down at

the magenta satin counterpane and studied it carefully, unwilling to meet the earl's eyes again. Why did the fates have to be so heartless? Why had they contrived to throw her into this man's house when just being in his presence made an ache start deep in her chest? And finally, why did he have to be so obliging and charming? She could have kept her defenses up against him much better if he were not.

CHAPTER 20

Caroline had dreaded her confrontation with Lord Devlon and now it was over, she considered, as she lay in the bed and stared at the ceiling. The patterns were unchanged; the old frescoes remained just as they had looked after her intense study of them this morning. She had also had a great deal of time to survey the green and tan wallpaper and dark green hangings on the window.

The heavy old pieces of dark furniture—a bureau, a desk, a lowboy, and chairs—had likewise been thoroughly examined. There was certainly time enough for her to see all there was of interest in the room. And she had long ago exhausted the interesting things. Now she watched the progress of a small black bug making its way across the ceiling. She wondered absently how the insect was able to walk upside down.

At present, she thought with a sigh, she would give anything just to walk at all, in any position. Of all the terrible afflictions to have, why must she have one that required the patient to lie so uncomfortably still?

And why, she wondered with a petulant look at

the door, did no one come to ask after her? It had been a solid hour since her maid had last looked in. She was certainly not a demanding patient, and she didn't think she had asked Clara to fluff the pillow too many times, but there had been a certain look of exasperation in that woman's face the last time she had performed the chore.

As to that, why did the earl not come to see her again? Since his visit late yesterday afternoon, he had not been back. And that had been a full sixteen-and-a-half hours ago. One would think he would consider it his duty as a host to look in on her from time to time. She moved with great care to shift to a slightly more comfortable position. Actually, she was sure she had exhausted all of the comfortable positions and all that remained were ones that made either her legs or back ache.

Caroline glanced up at the ceiling again and then reached for the hand bell on a table by the side of her bed. She believed she would just have Clara fluff the pillows once more. When her hand did not encounter the brass bell, she carefully turned her head to look at the stand. The bell, she noted with chagrin, was not there. Clara must have taken it with her.

She drew her hand back onto the bed and rehearsed the peal she would ring over her maid's head when that witless creature had the misfortune to appear. Caroline was not one to become pettish after a few hours of enforced rest—certainly not. But she was used to being obeyed by her maid. The very nerve of that woman leaving her without a bell! What if she had had a seizure and died? How would Clara have felt then?

Her thoughts were interrupted when the door opened and her maid appeared. "How's the patient?" she asked brightly.

"You took the bell with you!" Caroline accused.

"Why, it's there on your other pillow, miss," Clara replied, pointing.

Caroline moved her head slowly to see that the bell was indeed lying where it must have dropped when she had fallen asleep a while back.

"Were you needing me for something?"

"Yes. Please fluff the pillows. I can't believe these wretched things are made from feathers. I am persuaded they are stuffed with old rags tied in hard knots."

"I'm sure they are not," Clara said with strained patience as she bent to gently work the pillow.

"Has Lord Devlon asked after me?"

"Not that I am aware of. I think he left early this morning. No doubt he didn't wish to disturb you before he left."

"I would have been awake," Caroline pouted. "At least he could have left a message for me."

"Yes, miss. He could have. Why don't you just try to get some sleep," she suggested with an attempt at a sunny smile.

"I cannot sleep. I cannot do anything in this miserable position! No one can lie on his back endlessly, not even the dead. And that is what I shall certainly be if I am forced to remain like this much longer."

"Don't overset yourself. You know what the doctor said."

"That idiot with his bag of leeches! Well named, too, I should say. I wouldn't ask him to look after a drowned cat. If he is so mightily concerned about my health, then where is he?" Caroline directed a challenging look at her maid.

"Oh dear. I'm acting like a petulant child," she murmured, her fingers unconsciously rubbing the satin of the counterpane. "I'm sorry, I don't mean to fuss at you. It is only that I am so terribly frustrated and *bored*."

"I know. Let us hope your illness will not last much longer."

"Yes," Caroline agreed, disheartened. "Perhaps you could read to me for a time."

"Of course."

While Clara settled onto the chair beside her and began to read a gothic novel, Caroline's attention wandered. She could not endure much more time lying flat on her back in this house. Lord, she couldn't endure being in the house at all, let alone under these humiliating circumstances. Perhaps if another doctor were sent for he would know of a cure for her ailment. But Lord Devlon had not even complied with her request to find some sort of helpful medicine from the local chemist. Didn't anyone care that she was sick? she demanded of herself indignantly.

She was so lost in thought, she did not hear the door open or see the earl enter. He approached the bed quietly, his hands behind his back.

"Oh, look, miss. You have company." Clara turned to Lord Devlon. "She's very bored and a bit blue-deviled. She was just asking about you."

"Don't be ridiculous, Clara," Caroline said testily. "I'm in perfectly good spirits and I don't recall asking about the earl at all." If her words were rude, the cross frown that accompanied them did not bespeak any better for her temper.

The earl appeared oblivious to those signs as he drew his hands from behind his back and presented a bouquet of primroses. "I have brought you some flowers to enliven your room."

"Thank you," she mumbled.

"I'll put them in water." Clara's cheery voice overshadowed her mistress's rebellious one. She took the flowers and scampered from the room, leaving the door ajar.

"Now then," he turned back to her. "Are you better?"

Caroline looked up at the tall man standing over her bed. His black hair was still ruffled from the wind and he wore riding breeches, but his tan waistcoat and starched cravat looked clean and crisp. "I feel as well as can be expected," she said in the mournful accents of one who expects to die momentarily.

"That is good."

"Well it is not precisely what I would term 'good,' my lord," she flared, "when I am not able to move about or do anything for myself for fear of some very dreadful complications to my disease."

"What are the complications?" he asked mildly as he seated himself in the chair vacated by Clara. He picked up the book and glanced through it as he spoke.

He might at least give her the benefit of his full attention, Caroline fumed. She ought to ask him to leave. At the realization that she would be alone once again were she to do so, she softened her attitude toward him.

"Well, the doctor said he had known of at least two young ladies whose eyes had crossed because they had got up and moved about instead of lying in the bed as they were directed. I can hardly credit that, but I suppose there are some strange diseases. I mean, only look at the Blind Stagger. Why, cows just walk until they fall over dead. So, surely if animals can have such unusual diseases we can also. Although," she added, with a wistful look, "I should like to have the Blind Stagger just now, so I might walk instead of lying stiff on the bed."

"I daresay, you shall be well and up in a week," he predicted in rallying tones.

"I don't know," Caroline replied glumly. "The doctor did not even say if he would look in on me again. In fact, he was a most unusual sort of man."

"Yes, well," Lord Devlon cleared his throat and looked back at the book. "Ah, I see you have an interest in gothic novels."

"My maid does and she likes to read aloud." She wished he had found one of her improving books instead of a Mrs. Radcliffe novel.

"I see."

"But about the physician," she pressed. "I was rather dazed from the carriage accident when he examined me, but he seemed an odd sort of man. I don't know exactly how. He had a bit of a peculiar accent, rather lilting. Not like anything one hears in this part of the country."

"I believe I heard someone say he was from the north country," the earl supplied quickly.

"Oh, then that would account for his accent. But if he will not be coming back, I think you should have another doctor look at me."

Lord Devlon cleared his throat again and leafed through the book once more. "Yes, I will be going into town in a day or so, and I shall ask someone to come out and have a look at you."

Caroline stiffened at the negligent tone of his words. Didn't he even care enough about her health to see she obtained proper medical attention? People were so insensitive to the sick. She made a mental note to spend the remainder of her days visiting the ill should she survive this bout of the Red Ague.

"And another curious thing," she continued, struck by the name of her illness. "Have you ever even heard of the Red Ague? I own, I am not well versed in medicine, but I would think I should have heard the name of it. Are you familiar with it, my lord?"

"Er, yes. I knew a man once who had it."

"What happened to him?"

"I believe he stayed abed for the allotted time and he recovered quite satisfactorily."

"Who was he?"

"Just some neighbor." He waved his hand indifferently toward the window.

"Oh, someone around here?"

"Yes," he replied.

"Would you mind terribly sending for him? I would so like to talk to someone who has suffered from the disease. It would ease my mind no end; you really cannot imagine."

"I fear that is impossible. He is dead."

"Dead! You said he recovered."

"Well, he died some years later of a completely unconnected ailment."

"Oh," Caroline moved her head on the pillow and looked at her visitor. His eyes, friendly and concerned today, never seemed to meet hers directly. Perhaps her own eyes had already begun to cross and it made him uncomfortable to look at her.

"Would you bring me a hand mirror?" she asked.

Lord Devlon looked startled by such a request but rose to comply, returning from the dressing table a moment later with a gold-edged mirror, which he handed to her.

Caroline took it and peeped into it anxiously. Her eyes, she noted with relief, still looked normal with the hazel pupils where she had hoped they would be. And her face still retained its creamy complexion. All in all, she really didn't look sick.

"Thank you," she said as she handed the mirror back to him.

Lord Devlon took it wordlessly and placed it on his lap as he reseated himself.

For a moment neither spoke and Caroline was conscious of a feeling of uncomfortableness. Really, it was an embarrassing situation to be in. A man who had accused her of unspeakable things had been forced to take her into his home by a most curious set of coincidences. He, doubtless, felt as discomfited as she did.

Caroline broke the silence by saying, "I should contact my sister and tell her I will not be arriving in Devonshire, but I don't have her direction. She was to meet me in Exeter."

"I'm sure she isn't worried," he noted.

Caroline looked at him resentfully. "Whatever your personal feelings toward me may be, my lord, I assure you there are those in my family who feel concern for my safety. Of course she will worry when I do not arrive."

"Well, yes, I didn't precisely mean she wouldn't wonder. I only meant she would doubtless assume there was a logical explanation." The earl shifted in the chair. Deception, he was discovering, was not his forte. And it was damned hard to sit here and watch this healthy young woman lie in agonizing immobility because she believed dire events would take place if she moved.

"Surely it would not hurt anything if you just sat up in bed, or in a chair, for an hour or two," he offered. "I think it would improve your circulation."

Caroline looked at him coldly. "You cannot have my best interests in mind or you would not have suggested that, my lord. The doctor specifically said I was to lie flat."

"Of course. I only thought you would be more comfortable in a chair."

"Of course I would be more comfortable in a chair!

I would be more comfortable most anywhere but here! Why, I—" She got no further. The pent-up tears that had lurked beneath the surface since early this morning burst forth and she brought both hands to cover her face.

Lord Devlon stood hastily. "Don't cry, my dear. There now, it's not so very bad, is it?" he murmured gently as he rang for the maid. "Please, Caroline," he pleaded, "don't cry so. You'll make yourself ill." She was tearing him apart with her sobs of despair. He touched her hair reassuringly and silently cursed the baron for inflicting this torture on her.

CHAPTER 21

Caroline was vaguely conscious of voices around her, but the effort to open her eyes was too taxing. Instead she lay motionless, listening to the people speaking, and enjoying the delicious drifting sensation that surrounded her.

". . . laudanum . . . sleeping easier now," a woman's voice said in hushed tones.

"But Clara," a louder voice said, "do you really think you ought to?"

". . . crying . . . beside herself . . . had to . . ." came the whispered answer.

The sounds of doors opening and closing and then silence told Caroline her visitors had left. She put them totally from her mind to give herself over to floating along on a dreamy current of utter relaxation.

She must have wafted off to sleep again. When she gradually awoke, her mind seemed clearer; the fuzzy edges of an earlier time had been honed off. But she was so very tired still, as she lay with her eyes closed.

"I cannot think what she is doing here. When we left she and the earl were on the very worst of terms, and the letter Mama received from her was most unflattering toward him."

Caroline's eyes opened wide then and she found herself staring into the honest green ones of her niece. "Melissa, whatever are you doing here?"

"I'm on my way to Leicestershire," she explained simply. "How do you feel, Auntie Caro? Your maid said you had been in a carriage accident."

"Yes." Caroline dismissed such trivial matters to pursue the one of greater interest to her. "But why are *you* here?"

"I told you," Melissa repeated patiently, "I am bound for Leicestershire. The solicitor suggested I stop here first to settle some final matters."

Caroline closed her eyes again. Perhaps this was another of the series of dreams she had experienced since she had been confined to bed. When she opened her eyes again, doubtless she would discover her niece was gone and the room was empty. But when she raised her lashes, Melissa not only remained, but Annie was with her, bending toward Caroline with a worried look.

"I'm certain you're not being looked after properly. I have the very thing to revive you. It's a mixture of secret herbs," she confided.

"I think she is tired," Melissa said, gently pulling the maid away from the bedside. "I shall return later, Auntie Caro, when you are more in health and wish to talk."

"Wait!" Caroline stopped her just before she stepped outside the door. "What did you say about a solicitor?"

"Oh, when the earl came to Ireland and I confessed I had taken the treasures, he said all was forgiven. He means to provide me with a place to live and to make amends to you also." She smiled happily and closed the door.

Caroline stared dazedly after her, trying to piece together the complicated pieces of the puzzle and having no luck. What had Melissa meant about taking the heirlooms? And why was the earl providing her with anything? He had established beyond doubt, he was under no obligation to do so.

It was all so terribly complicated, she fretted. She was just accustoming herself to her own plight, and now there were new things to understand, and her mind was blurring again.

Caroline was roused from her tossing and turning by a kind voice inducing her to drink some water and murmuring soothing words while she did so. Then she fell into another cloud-edged sleep where reality and unreality seemed to converge and weave themselves together.

When she awoke to the crisp light of late afternoon, she realized she must have been asleep for a very long time. And the events she recalled surely were all parts of a dream. At one point she had even thought she had felt the touch of a large, masculine hand laid gently on her cheek. Who would have done so? No, of course she had imagined it.

The door opened quietly and Clara entered. "Oh, you're awake. Lord Devlon is in the sitting room and wishes to see you. Will you receive him?"

"Yes, of course." She hastily pulled her nightcap

from her head and patted her curls. "Does my hair look presentable?" she asked anxiously.

"It looks very fine," Clara assured her and left to escort the earl in.

He entered with a tentative smile on his lips. Caroline smiled back at him, unaware she did so—she was so intent on studying his face. He really did look most handsome, she thought, with those deep blue eyes and that roguish dimple set in his rugged face.

"I am pleased you consented to see me, Miss Norton. I did not mean to overset you the other day, and I promise I shan't do so again."

"I fear my nerves were a bit overwrought then from lying still so long."

He seated himself on the chair by the bed. "Are you feeling much improved?"

"Yes, my lord." Caroline wished she had put on her new lime-green nightdress instead of this cream muslin one he had seen before. Of course, the covers were pulled up to her neck and he could only see the lace, but the lace on the green nightdress was ever so much nicer.

"Miss Norton," he continued, suddenly grave, "you and I have not always dealt well together, but I want you to know I have a profound respect for you. In short, Miss Norton, my feelings toward you are so altered from what they were when I first met you that I feel I could make so bold as to attach the word—"

"I have found it!" Annie cried, bursting into the room and interrupting Lord Devlon just as he reached to touch Caroline's hand, which lay atop the covers.

Caroline could have killed her. She had been breathlessly awaiting the earl's next word, but he straightened and bowed formally at the maid's entrance. "I shall call on you later, Miss Norton. I see you have other visitors."

"It was very hard to come by, don't think it was not," Annie informed them as she began setting an assortment of jars on the stand by Caroline's bed. "But I knew you would not rest easy until I came to your aid. Stay, my lord, don't leave on my account. This won't be a minute and then you can go back to exchanging commonplaces with her. I'm certain she wants company, she is so very pale and fretful."

"Her cheeks are quite flushed." He bowed again. "Servant," he said briskly and left the room.

"Why did you have to come in *now?*" Caroline demanded irritably, turning a sullen face to Annie.

"Well, I couldn't make it back from the village any sooner, or I certainly would have been here before this," Annie assured her. "Let me see," she mumbled to herself, "I'll just need a dash of this and . . ."

Caroline turned away from Annie and tried to savor again the moment when Lord Devlon had looked intently into her eyes. What had he been about to say? It had sounded for all the world as if he meant to make a declaration. She sighed and smiled blissfully.

"Here it is," Annie announced.

Caroline meekly allowed the maid to give her the mixture, since there seemed to be no other way to rid the room of her. As Annie turned to leave, Caroline called after her, "Please tell his lordship I am not occupied now if he wishes to see me again."

Annie nodded and left, returning moments later to announce he was busy with company and would doubtless be unable to see her the rest of the evening. "It is already quite seven thirty, and I don't doubt they mean to stay for dinner."

"Most inconvenient!" Caroline fretted.

"Indeed it is," the older woman commiserated, "but that baron and Miss Georgiana do take some starts. It's hard to say how long they mean to stay."

"Who?" Caroline demanded.

"Why, Melissa's mother and the baron. They arrived earlier this afternoon, all smiles and cooing. They're to be married."

"How did Georgiana discover I was here? I didn't even know where she was in Devonshire to send a message to her."

"Devonshire?" Annie looked perplexed. "They haven't been to Devonshire. They came over from Ireland with Melissa, and I and they have been in the neighborhood the whole of the time you have been ill." She closed the door behind her.

Georgiana had been near here, Caroline puzzled. Then why had she not come to see her? In point of fact, this was just one more of the many mysteries that had occurred since she had set out for Devonshire. But a pattern was taking shape in her mind, and she did not at all like what it revealed.

Two persons' names recurred with uncomfortable regularity in her cataloging of the events that had befallen her since leaving Wiltshire; and they were Georgiana's and Lord Devlon's. After all, it had been at her sister's request she had begun her journey to Devonshire. Now she learned Georgiana had not even been in Devonshire. And how extremely singular Caroline should have a carriage accident so very close to Lord Devlon's house. Even more odd was the fact a doctor had happened by so shortly after the event.

Caroline sat straight up in bed at the thought of the doctor. How had she been so excessively stupid as not to have realized who he must be. He was the baron, of course! And his accent, the one she had been trying so hard to place and the one Lord Devlon had told her was a north-country accent, was, of course, an Irish brogue.

The earl had deliberately lied to her. He had obviously had a hand in arranging this whole masquerade. He *had* been most anxious to see her. When she had denied his requests, she fumed, he must have decided to bring her to him since she would not permit him to visit her. He was an odious, strong-willed man who was bent on having his own way in all things. But why? What did he want from her?

That question had no sooner entered her mind than she recalled his earlier visit to her. He had been going to say something of a most particular nature, of that she was certain. In fact, she suspected he had meant to declare himself, and she had wanted him to.

How could she have been so dull-witted? If the earl meant to offer for her, it could only be to compensate for his earlier behavior. After all, he had written in his letter that he owed her something. And Melissa had said he wanted to make amends to her. It had all been for the most elevating of motives, she railed, that of easing his guilty conscience. Just because he had said a few gentle words to her and called her "Caroline" when she broke down crying meant nothing. Certainly not that he loved her.

Well, she wouldn't have him! In fact, she would not stay here one minute longer than need be, she vowed, throwing back the covers and jumping out of the bed. She changed from her nightdress into a serviceable walking gown of dove gray and sat down in a chair, still fuming. She would tell Lord Devlon exactly what she thought of his unforgivable machinations the first thing in the morning. Imagine him keeping her confined to bed with the Banbury tale she had a rare illness? Whose idea was that, she wondered angrily. Lord Devlon had certainly shored up the belief with the facile lie he knew a man who had had the same disease. Tomorrow, she promised herself, she was leaving this house and the detestable earl behind forever. The Red Ague, indeed!

While she sat in the chair the hours slipped by, noted only by the Spanish clock in the hall downstairs. Slowly Caroline's plans changed and she made the rueful admission that she might be able to make a grand departure from the house, but she would then look excessively foolish walking down the road to the village. And since her own carriage was being repaired, she had no other way to leave. She certainly did not intend to ask the earl for the use of his.

No, she resigned herself, there was only one way

for her to quit Hollowsby, and that was in the first light of morning when no one was about. She would walk to the village—it couldn't be more than an hour's trek, she reckoned—and there she would board the Exeter *Fly* and return to Wiltshire. Drat, why was she crying? She dashed a tear from her face and straightened in the chair.

But the tears continued to roll down her cheeks in spite of her resolution not to cry. She couldn't help it; she felt so miserable. For some reason that followed no logic whatsoever, she had fallen in love with Lord Devlon. She tried to kindle a dislike for him by recalling the underhanded way he had plotted to bring her to Hollowsby against her wishes, but it was useless. That thought kept slipping to the back of her mind to be replaced by one of him trying to console her when she was upset and calling her "Caroline." The tears flowed faster, and she brought a handkerchief to her nose. If only things had happened differently. But she couldn't marry him under these circumstances; she would be even more desolate knowing that he was being a martyr. She didn't want him to sacrifice himself for her; she wanted him to love her. Caroline stifled a sob and rocked herself slowly back and forth on the chair. She must be firm. She must leave as soon as it was light or she would surely abandon her plan altogether and throw herself into his arms.

When the first tentative strokes of dawn filtered into the room, Caroline steeled herself to put her plan into action. She rolled a few of her clothes into a bundle, tied them with a satin sash, and walked out of the room and down the hall.

Stopping at the next room, she roused her maid. "Clara," she shook her briskly. "I don't know whether or not you are a party to this outrageous scheme, but we are leaving."

Clara blinked uncertainly. "Ma'am?" she said groggily. "Shouldn't you be in bed?"

"Of course I should! Any decent body should at this hour, but I am not allowed that luxury."

The maid raised herself on one elbow, glanced toward the window and then back to Caroline. "It is just now light," she reported.

"I know that. I didn't wake you to find out the time. I am ready to leave, and you are coming with me."

"Now?"

"Yes, now," she returned implacably.

Clara rose slowly, looking quizzically at her mistress from time to time as she dressed under Caroline's stern eye and packed her small valise. Then she trudged out into the hall and down the steps to the rotunda.

As they let themselves out the front door, Clara agonized over what to do. She was forming the strong suspicion Caroline's affliction had affected her brain; she wasn't at all certain she should not be physically restraining her mistress from leaving. But one glance at her companion's stony face decided her it would be a futile gesture. Better to humor her for the present. Perhaps in time Caroline would regain her composure, realize what she was about, and return to the house.

"I want you to tell me everything you know," Caroline said abruptly after they were some distance from the house.

"About what?" Clara asked blankly.

"Don't try to fob me off with innocence. I may not be awake on all suits—I have obviously been very hen-witted on a great many lately—but I have belatedly come to my senses."

Clara, who was of the opinion Caroline might have lost her senses altogether, plodded along silently.

"Well?" Caroline demanded imperiously. "What part had you in this affair? Did you know the coachman was supposed to wreck us?"

"Indeed not!"

Caroline looked at her sharply. No, she realized, it was doubtful Clara had known. She would hardly have consented to be a party to a deed that could have done them both a serious harm. "Never mind," she said softly. "It doesn't signify."

This quick change from anger to calmness only made Clara the more uncertain of the state of Caroline's mind. But really, she concluded as she marched along, there was nothing for it but to go wherever her mistress went.

CHAPTER 22

Lord Devlon was in a very good humor as he sat at the breakfast table and looked out the casement window to a bluish-gray kestrel hovering in the sky. He was recalling Miss Norton's charmingly natural smile of yesterday. He had been surprised by such a warm reception. It had, perhaps, accounted for why he said things he might not have spoken otherwise, but he had no regrets. He only wished her maid had not interrupted before he could complete the whole of his question, although he had already seen the answer in Caroline's eyes. They would formalize their plans today.

"My lord, I do not know what is to be done!" Annie cried, flying into the room and standing before him wringing her hands and babbling incoherently. "When I gave her the draft it was to make the *illness* disappear, but I did not think it would be so very effective it would make *her* disappear. I should have tried it on that troublesome dog, had I known."

The earl turned toward this unwelcome distraction. "If something is amiss, please inform the butler. He is very capable of handling any problems."

"But not this! She is gone."

He was instantly alert, sitting bolt upright in his chair. "What the devil are you talking about? Who is gone?"

"Miss Norton, of course. I only took her something yesterday to help her along in her recovery and now—"

The earl heard no more. He was out of the room and heading up the steps. Reaching Caroline's room, he pushed the door open without bothering to knock. Inside her bedroom he could see the signs of hasty packing. And on her bedside stand, he noted with a curiously deflated look, were the flowers he had brought her, jammed upside down into their vase.

Annie entered behind him, looking woebegone.

"What did you say to her last evening?" he asked, still steadily regarding the flowers.

"Why, very little. She was quite confused, my lord. She was speaking of going to Devonshire to see Miss Georgiana, which is utter nonsense because Miss Georgiana was never there."

"I see." He did too. Caroline had deduced exactly what was going forward and had been less than pleased with what she saw. "Damn!" he muttered aloud, crossing to the window and angrily jerking back the dark green curtain to look out. Why had he not told her of her sister's scheme before she discovered it on her own? She was bound to be angry now, and who was to say where she might go?

But whichever direction she headed, there was only one place to meet the stage and that was at the village. He stalked from the room and down the steps calling loudly to have his horse saddled.

Moments later he set off toward the village, riding at breakneck speed, and rehearsing in his mind what to say to induce Caroline to return to Hollowsby with him. The words to accomplish that purpose, he feared, would be hard indeed to find. Unless he was sorely mistaken, she would be in a royal fit of temper.

Lord Devlon's assessment of Caroline's humor was most accurate. She had boarded the carriage that morning to settle herself between Clara and a large, middle-aged, apple-eating woman. On the seat facing her in the uncomfortable coach was a thin man dressed in farmer's clothes of drab brown. He occupied himself casting sour glances on the three women facing him. Next to him was a brightly smiling young girl who prattled on about the relative she was going to visit.

Caroline nudged back in the seat to regain the space the apple-eater was usurping and closed her eyes. The best thing for her to do, she considered wearily, was to fall asleep and escape her present company and the unbidden, unhappy thoughts that crowded into her mind.

She was prevented from accomplishing that purpose when the carriage came to an abrupt halt and the sound of voices could be heard outside. A moment later the door opened and a finely dressed gentleman appeared—Lord Devlon.

"Miss Norton," he greeted her, "if you would be so good as to step down, I wish to speak to you."

Caroline's initial gladness invoked by the sight of

him was dampened almost immediately by the memory of his actions. "I am far too busy just now, my lord," she snapped.

He gave her a look of exasperation, closed the door, and the sound of voices was heard again. Then Lord Devlon reappeared and entered the coach, seating himself on the bench seat across from her, between the sour old man and the young girl. He looked wholly out of place in his biscuit-hued breeches, dark blue Weston coat and York tan driving gloves, but he seemed not to notice that as he placed his riding crop across his knees and settled back on the seat.

"Pray, what are you doing, my lord?" Caroline asked with dignity.

"I am a passenger," he grinned. "Now the coach may continue on its way, while we are free to have our discussion."

She tilted her face away from him. "I scarcely see what you and I can have to talk about."

"On the contrary, we have a great deal."

The interested eyes of Clara, the young girl, the older woman, the farmer, and the earl all focused on Caroline, awaiting her response and making her extremely uncomfortable.

"This is most unseemly," she bristled. "A common stage is hardly the place to have a discussion such as this."

"I quite agree," he smiled pleasantly, "but since you would not alight so I might speak to you in private, I am forced to pay my addresses in public."

"You aiming to offer for that wench?" the thin man beside the earl interrupted him.

"I am," he replied evenly.

"Take my advice, don't do it."

The woman seated next to Caroline suspended her apple in the act of bringing it to her mouth and stared in astonishment. "But look at her dress! And she's carrying the rest of her clothes tied in a bundle. She's not in your class at all, m'lord," she advised the earl kindly.

"She is a very fine lady," Clara riposted, outraged.

"I quite agree," Lord Devlon agreed, "and I think she will make a superb wife."

"I lost my wife three months ago," the farmer offered.

"How sad for you," the young girl said with feeling.

"Not a bit of it. She ran off with my best friend, Henry. Sad for him, I should say. Take my word for it, m'lord, don't leg-shackle yourself. Women do nothing but lead a fellow a merry chase. Never know what they're thinking," he grumbled.

"Miss Norton," Lord Devlon directed his eyes toward her, "will you do me the honor of marrying me?"

"Certainly not!" she said crisply. "I have been abominably used by you. I can only hope, since you are aboard this coach, that you have not arranged for it to overturn also."

He laughed easily, "Is that why you left Hollowsby? I did not plan that little incident, Miss Norton. Your sister did."

"I don't believe you," she fired rudely. "Why should she do such a thing?"

"Because she fancies you have a certain affection for me, which could mature into something much more were you to allow it to do so."

"How romantic," the girl rhapsodized. "I should have him. He is very tall and most handsome. I doubt you would find another such as he were you to reject him."

Caroline found occupation regarding the hands she held tightly clenched in her lap. He had not been responsible for bringing her to Hollowsby? She wavered in her resolve to dislike him. Still she shored up her failing animosity; there was the matter of the way he had treated her when she had first met him.

"My lord, we would not suit. You have called me some unspeakable things."

"Like what?" the farmer asked with interest.

Caroline gave him a withering look and turned back to the earl. "I don't wish to talk of the matter any further. If you will kindly leave, I will not be forced to look at you, an event that would give me no end of satisfaction."

"I don't know. I think he has a right pleasing countenance," the woman beside her remarked. She smiled sweetly at the earl. "I am not married," she told him graciously.

He returned a kind smile. "I'm very sensible of your charm, madame, but I rather had my heart set on Miss Norton. You see, I am quite in love with her."

"Then, why do you not tell her?" the girl suggested. "I think it will make all the difference in the world in your suit."

"Do you?" he asked politely. He turned back to Caroline. "Would my saying I am top-over-tail in love with you alter your strong aversion to me?"

Caroline avoided his eyes and looked toward the window. "You cannot mean it, my lord."

"But I assure you, I do."

"You'll be sorry," the thin man promised ominously.

"Do be quiet," Clara snapped. "She is just about to accept him."

"I am not!" Caroline denied.

"Oh, yes you are," Clara said. "I can always tell when you are weakening. And you might as well have him, you know, since you will be miserable without him."

"I shall be perfectly happy without him," Caroline asserted with haughty pride.

"Miss Norton, I shall do my utmost to see that you never want for anything, and I believe I can offer you a tolerably comfortable life. I wish you will consider my offer."

"If she decides against you, m'lord . . ." the woman beside Caroline hinted.

"You are most kind, madame, but as I have said, I am rather partial to Miss Norton. Since I have never before offered for a woman, it may only be my approach she objects to."

"Well, very few men do make declarations in coaches," Caroline remarked, her eyes downcast.

"I am aware of that. I am perfectly willing to

debark, if you will, and we can discuss the matter at greater length."

"Yes, do," the girl enthused, reaching up and pulling the check string as she spoke.

The coach came to a halt and Lord Devlon stepped down, then reached a hand up to assist Caroline. She vacillated a moment but stepped daintily down at the farmer's muttered recommendation Lord Devlon should not do anything so foolish as to tie himself to a shrew. He assisted Clara down and untied his horse, leaving the coach free to drive off with the occupants expressing their opinions as they left.

Taking Caroline's arm, Lord Devlon led her a short distance away from Clara, then turned to face her. Without speaking, he reached down to untie the pale blue satin ribbons of her dark blue hat.

"What are you doing?" she demanded, her eyes intently held to a green leaf on a tree just past the earl's head.

"I am taking your bonnet off," he replied as he executed the action, "so that I may kiss you better."

As he brought his lips to hers she didn't make the smallest protest. In fact, she found more than a little satisfaction in the calm but thorough way he kissed her. And while his lips searched hers his hands stole around her back and supported her in a strong clasp as he drew her ever closer to him. It was highly improper and utterly delicious. Caroline was not certain she would ever have pulled away, but the earl finally released her with obvious reluctance and pulled back slightly.

The pounding of hooves signaling the arrival of another carriage registered in Caroline's mind, but she did not turn to look. She was staring happily up into the earl's deep blue eyes and liking what she saw there.

"I do believe they have managed without my help," Georgiana approved.

"Famous!" Melissa joined in. "I have wonderful news, Auntie Caro. Clover is to be a father, and I shall give you one of his pups as a wedding present."

Lord Devlon's eyes never wavered from Caroline's face as he replied, "Miss Norton has not yet said she will have me."

"Oh, she will," Georgiana assured him airily. "But we will leave you to persuade her. Do come with us," she exhorted Clara. The maid boarded their carriage, and they were off in a cloud of dust, leaving Caroline and the earl standing alone once again at the side of the road.

"Your sister seems to still be of the opinion you will marry me," he said quietly.

"Do you know," Caroline mused, "before I left Trevina's house to go to Hollowsby for the first time, I told her I should marry the first man who was not shocked by my sister's irregular way of life. Are you shocked, my lord?"

"No. Does that mean you will have me?"

"I shall think on it," she said primly and was prevented from saying anything further when Lord Devlon caught her up in a kiss that was even more breathtaking and demanding than the first. And equally as enjoyable, Caroline considered as her eyes slowly flitted open.

"Are you through thinking?" he asked as he released her, "or do you need more incentive to help you make up your mind?"

"You can be most persuasive, my lord. And I *did* promise Trevina. It would not be seemly to go back on my word, would it?"

"It would not," he agreed gravely.

"Then I suppose there is nothing for it. I am constrained to marry you."

"You are most obliging," he murmured.

"I know," she agreed, turning her face up to his. "Now I think you must kiss me before we begin the walk back to Hollowsby."

He obeyed graciously and at length. It was some minutes before they parted. "It is not necessary to walk, my love; I have my horse."

"Yes, but I don't think I shall be able to sit or lie comfortably for some time."

"Let us hope it is a situation that is remedied before our marriage takes place," he said as he took her arm and they began the ten-mile walk back to the estate, discussing their wedding plans as they went.